THIS SPECIAL SIGNED EDITION IS
LIMITED TO 1000 NUMBERED COPIES.

THIS IS COPY 845.

MICHAEL MARSHALL SMITH

TIME OUT

TIME OUT

MICHAEL MARSHALL SMITH

Subterranean Press 2024

Time Out
Copyright © 2024
by Michael Marshall Smith.
All rights reserved.

Dust jacket illustration
Copyright © 2024
by Samuel Araya.
All rights reserved.

Interior design
Copyright © 2024
by Desert Isle Design, LLC.
All rights reserved.

First Edition

ISBN
978-1-64524-159-1

Subterranean Press
PO Box 190106
Burton, MI 48519

subterraneanpress.com

Manufactured in the United States of America

1

I FIRST SUSPECTED serious issues with our marriage when my wife called me an asshole on Christmas Day. She said it quietly but with enormous intensity, in the kitchen, away from the ears of the daughter I'd just told I was too busy to play with. In my defense, lunch on Christmas Day is my responsibility, always has been. It's a complex meal with a lot of moving parts. You can't just abandon it for half an hour to lie on the floor and build Legos. I'll admit however that I'd been dipping into a bottle of wine during the initial cooking process and probably hadn't spoken to Emily with the patience she expected or deserved. I'd already realized this. I was in fact heading to the living room to reassure her that I'd be totally down for hanging out after lunch when I encountered Leela in the kitchen doorway. Arms tightly folded. Looking at me. It was not a kind look. I asked what her facial expression meant. That's when she called me an asshole.

I responded somewhat in kind, explaining how busy I was. Unfortunately the hand gesture designed to demonstrate the many dishes I had in progress knocked my wine glass off the counter. It broke, of course, because God hates me, sending a lurid splash of red across the floor. I stopped talking.

Leela looked at me a moment longer, judging that her point had been made, and went in the other room to play with Emily.

I poured more wine. Cleaned up the broken glass, suffering a minor cut. Calmed down. Went back to cooking.

LUNCH WAS FINE, though quiet. We moved to Santa Cruz three years ago. Our families live on the other side of the country, a journey we make for Thanksgiving, so Christmas is just the three of us. Emily did her best to thaw the atmosphere and we did play with Legos later and I think we had a pretty good time, though I eventually started to doze. I woke a few hours later to find myself sprawled sideways on the couch. Child and wife had gone to bed.

I finished clearing up the kitchen, packed away the leftovers, and followed upstairs. Emily was asleep in her room. I quietly wished her goodnight anyway.

Leela was a motionless shape in our bed, her back toward me. I did not try to engage her in conversation. She was either asleep or firmly presenting as such. I knew from experience that talk is sometimes better left until tomorrow, and the period spent crashed out in the living room had left me with both a headache and the glum realization that the day had not gone as well as it should, and any objective observer would pin the blame on me. It didn't matter that I'd been working hard up until six the previous evening, this day a brief pause in relentless deadlines. I'd been an asshole.

I drank a lot of water and went to sleep, hoping Emily at least enjoyed the Legos part, and had not gone to bed sad.

2

I WOKE LATE next morning, after nine, stirred from a deep sleep by the thud-thud-thud of a squirrel running down the top of our garden fence on Carol's side—an event so common that Leela and I referred to it as the "squirrel highway". Last night's gulped water and unscheduled pre-bed nap had mitigated the wine but I still did not feel on great form. Nonetheless I fashioned my face into a smile and turned toward my wife, determined to make up for the day before, starting with an offer of coffee in bed.

She wasn't there. This wasn't a complete surprise. She usually gets up before eight. But it was the day after Christmas, a day she refers to as "Boxing Day" because of English parents, and insists on taking easy. Either way, she was up. Maybe, I hoped, doing exactly what I'd been intending: waiting until I was awake to bring in some coffee as the start of a period of apology (on my part) and forgiveness (on hers)—after which we could get back into the groove of family life and what was left of the festive season.

I lay back, waited. Gave it fifteen minutes.

Got up.

I WAS NOT greeted in the kitchen by the smell of freshly-brewed hot beverage, nor by any sign of my wife. By "sign" I mean both that she was not physically present, and the kitchen remained in the state of clinical tidiness I'd left it the night before. This would be unlikely if Leela had spent even five minutes in there. I love the woman but her process with the arrangements of objects in any given space is fundamentally chaotic. I have mentioned this in the past but it was met by an immediate counter-strike detailing the much larger number of practical tasks she accomplishes around the house. I have not returned to the subject. I just tidy up. Not least because she is, of course, right.

I rested the back of my hand against the kettle. Cold. Overnight cold. Surprising. She doesn't wake up with her hand out grasping for caffeine, as I do, but generally wants some before long, and will default to instant coffee—a weirdly

TIME OUT

un-American habit which is doubtless also related to her parentage.

I went out the back door and into the garden. 'Leela?'

No reply. Our back yard is large, half an acre, a pool close to the house, the rest on a couple of levels and artfully divided by hedges high enough to stop you seeing into the next section. So if she wasn't going to answer, I had to visit each in turn.

I did so. No sign. I belatedly realized that when I'd opened the door from the kitchen, it had been locked. As I'd left it the night before. You can't do that from the outside. So she couldn't have been out here. Duh. It was clear I needed caffeine, stat.

I poured a glass of water while coffee perked. Stood sipping it looking out into the garden. I was a little pissed, though I wasn't sure why. It felt like some kind of point was being made, and not subtly. Obviously I was going to be sorry for what happened yesterday. So why make it hard for me to apologize?

Then I thought: *Emily*.

I checked the wall clock. Nine forty-five. Surprising she wasn't up and in the living room, playing with gifts from the day before, anxious for input and company. Unless perhaps she'd taken some key prizes upstairs when she went to bed… Of course.

That's where Leela would be. Hanging with her daughter on "Boxing Day morning". Hopefully not bad-mouthing me.

I poured two cups of coffee and took them upstairs, reaching again for a smile. When I got to Emily's room I nudged the door open with my foot, something cheerful on my lips.

But they weren't there.

3

I PAUSED, THEN turned on my heel, feeling slightly ridiculous with a cup of coffee in each hand. Back in the kitchen I put them on the counter, grabbed my phone and told Siri to call my wife. Chances were she wouldn't answer. But I could leave a message. And it would be polite. Because—

I paused my internal monologue, lowered the phone from my ear, cocked my head. Listened. I could hear ringing. A phone. Sounded like one of those old school rotary phones. After a moment, it stopped. The call on my own phone had gone to voicemail.

I didn't leave a message. Told Siri to ring Leela again. I knew what was going to happen because I recognized the ring tone, but wanted a directional fix. It was easy to track down and I got there before it went to voicemail a second time.

My wife's phone was on the charger on her nightstand.

MICHAEL MARSHALL SMITH

I stared at it until it stopped ringing. Leela listens to a *lot* of NPR. Keeps up with people on Facebook. Will get political on Twitter. Keeps an eye on what Emily's doing on Instagram, making sure it's within tolerance for an eleven-year-old. Reads the *Post* and anything new on the *New Yorker* every single day. As a consequence and given all these activities take place via her phone, it's pretty much never more than a few feet away from her.

I hesitated on the landing, and called Leela's name. Then Emily's. The house sounded very quiet.

I walked down the stairs and opened the front door. You can see the drive from there. Both cars were still there.

HALF AN HOUR later I was showered and dressed and in the kitchen and drinking more coffee. I'd also smoked a cigarette in the garden, although—in a settlement negotiated with wife and child—I wasn't supposed to until after five p.m. I'm allowed to vape, discreetly, but not actually smoke. But they weren't here, so.

In the meantime I'd figured it out.

They'd gone for a hike.

TIME OUT

Our house is on a hill near the edge of town. There's a gate at the top of the street giving access to a substantial wild area that includes oak and redwood forests and eventually segues into the lower reaches of the Santa Cruz mountains. I'd never really taken to the area despite some nice views over the bay. Leela is a fan, however, and it was conceivable she'd bounced out of bed, decided a walk was just the ticket—apparently it's traditional on Boxing fucking Day in jolly old England—and taken Emily with her. Mom and daughter bonding time. She hadn't taken her phone because she didn't want to be distracted, perhaps especially by her boorish husband.

It was the only thing that made sense. They wouldn't have gone downtown because it's a half-hour walk, and a lot more coming back, as every step is uphill on the return. No way Emily would have been up for that.

So…what did I do? I could sit it out. Do some work or prep lunch or whatever. Though kind of early for the latter. And I didn't especially want to work. And I felt too keyed up to sit and read. I had an apology ready in my head, carefully judged to cede ground on the ways in which I'd been an asshole without opening the door to the idea that the condition was universal. The Leela part of it would be fine. Probably. And I did want to see my daughter.

I could go meet them.

I didn't know which way they'd have gone, of course, and Leela leaving her phone behind prevented me from using Find My Friend. But—especially with a young non-hiker in tow—Leela would have stuck to the one of the main paths, judging the route so it'd be a nice walk without getting long or arduous enough to try a child's patience. Worst case I could walk up to the top of the road and wait at the gate (perhaps grabbing another sneaky cigarette, though I'd need to find some mints to take afterward, and it would leave me without any left, never a great feeling if you're addicted to nicotine). Stand there looking chilled and friendly and very much a man looking forward to the return of his beloved family.

Yeah, that worked. I hunted down some mints and took the last cigarette out of the pack—along with another cup of coffee. I had no idea how long I'd have to wait.

Thus armed, I left the house.

4

I LIKE TO walk. It's one of the few forms of exercise I actively enjoy—though I prefer there to be a goal at the end, like a coffee shop, bookstore or bar. My family counted as a goal, especially as I was starting to feel unnerved by their absence on the back of the disagreement the day before. By the time I'd got to the sidewalk my legs were waking up and I was distracted by wondering whether I should Plan A it and actually try to find them, keep going into the woods instead of stopping at the gate, in which case having a coffee cup with me would be a pain.

But then I stopped walking. Took me a second to work out why.

The good folks of Santa Cruz love time in nature, be it strolling the beach or surfing or some wholesome activity in the land you can access from the top of our street. One of the side effects of our house's position, therefore, is frequent foot traffic. You see cars going up and down the road too, though not many: parking is restricted so it's mainly local residents. Most people head up to the woods on foot or mountain bikes or trailing a dog or two behind. As a result it's pretty rare to stand in our house for five minutes without seeing someone heading up or down the hill, especially on a day when many people aren't at work and take the chance to do something hearty and outdoorsy instead.

I looked up the road.

Turned 180 degrees and looked down.

Nobody. In either direction. Right to the cross street, Borland, over three hundred yards away. Simple probability, maybe—but I knew part of me had been working at this before I consciously clocked it. Our house has two big windows on the street side of the living room. They take up most of the wall. In going back and forth through the house—looking for Leela or checking Emily's room, to get showered, or going back to the kitchen—I'd passed them a dozen times. Some part of my brain, diligent drone in the department that keeps track of shit I'm not consciously noting, was confident I hadn't glimpsed a passer-by in all that time.

I looked once more up the hill toward the gate. Still nobody. No cars had come down the road. The thought of cars made me pause, and focus on my senses. It was *very* quiet. I'd noticed this in the

TIME OUT

house earlier but assumed it was merely the lack of family sounds.

It was quiet out here, too. Almost silent. A rustle from leaves high in the trees. A bird tweeted, briefly but with great enthusiasm. The faintest of sounds that had to be the waves, a mile and a half away. Surf must be up. We heard the ocean here only infrequently and on the quietest of nights. Something else we could hear in those conditions—conditions like now, in fact—was traffic on Highway 17, the busy and twisty route over the mountains to San Jose and Silicon Valley, in use 24/7. It's about a mile from our house. And there was no sound from it.

I sipped a little coffee to make the cup easier to carry without spilling, and headed up the hill. After thirty yards there's a side road on the right. No movement along there. After another thirty, a curving road on the left—the last before town stops. No movement either. No people, no cars, no Amazon delivery trucks. The latter almost struck me as the most unusual thing.

I got to the gate, looked out over the land. Then turned back and stared down the long hill. Nothing. Nobody, anywhere.

Then, something. A squirrel came bounding out of the bushes on the left. Bounced halfway across the road, spotted something it liked the look of, investigated it. Ultimately rejected it as non-food, sat up a moment on its hind legs, before ambling across to the other side, as if it had all the time in the world.

Squirrels aren't dumb.

I got out my phone. Wasn't sure who to try. I work remotely and don't have a whole lot of friends in town. One possibility dropped quickly into my head, but it was a terrible idea. The fact it even occurred to me, after all this time, was an indication of how disconcerted I was starting to feel.

Then I thought of Mark—father of one of Emily's pals. We got on okay and met for a beer once in a while. Were overdue, in fact. Normally we set up such events by text but a call wouldn't be *too* weird. I could wish him Happy Christmas, and so on. I speed-dialed his number. Did not get the sound of ringing. Ended the call, tried again. Again, it didn't ring.

I flipped over to my recent calls and pressed an entry at random. The auto shop where the car had been serviced two days ago. I wasn't sure they'd be open the day after Christmas, but it didn't matter, as again I didn't get a ringing sound.

Next I pressed Leela's number—last dialed at 09:49. Again nothing. This was making no sense. I'd called the damned thing...

TIME OUT

Belatedly I realized the icon on the Recent slot for Leela's number showed the phone had automatically routed itself via Wi-Fi, as we'd been on the same home network at the time. That had worked. Using the actual phone system did not.

I remembered I'd brought the cigarette with me. Smoked it while watching the road below. Didn't bother with a mint.

I saw nothing. Nobody.

5

FIRST THING I did when I got home was try calling my phone from Leela's. In an expression of marital collegiality we have the same phone PIN. I got the same result as when trying to call hers from outside the house: she doesn't have hers set to re-route via Wi-Fi if available. Attempting a random number from her recents didn't work either.

I loaded Mail on my phone. A graphic wheel went around for a while but no new messages came in. It was possible there simply weren't any, but people tend to bug me on a regular basis and even on the day after Christmas there's bound to be newsletters urging you to celebrate the birth of our savior through buying things… I clicked the CNN app. It tried to serve up news for a while but eventually bailed to a white screen. Same with the *New York Times*. The App Store said it couldn't contact the server.

I got the same results from my laptop. Wi-Fi was working fine *within* the house—hence Leela's phone ringing earlier—but its connection to the outside world was down.

As was the phone network.

Okay, so what the *fuck*? One or other being out, sure. Comcast goes splat once in a while. Verizon gets blinky too—as noted, we're at the edge of town. But two unrelated companies, at the same time? Only explanation I could think of was a massive local power outage, but the lights in the kitchen were on. And the coffee machine still worked, thank god. Power was not the problem.

I sat in the living room, two phones and the laptop on the couch beside me. Meanwhile, nobody walked past the house outside. No cars went by. Then I thought:

Carol.

We hadn't had a lot of communication with our next-door neighbor—a pleasant-enough academic in her late sixties—but relations were cordial. A chat over the fence once in a while. She was the obvious next step. Knock on her door and see if she was having infrastructure challenges too. She might be freaked out and be grateful for the offer of help. Or reassurance, anyway, as I wasn't sure I had any solutions.

TIME OUT

Her car was in the drive but knocking on her door four times over a ten-minute period did not rouse a response. Yes of course she could be out on foot. She could be out of town.

But.

I walked out into the middle of the street. Still couldn't hear any traffic, anywhere. I headed into the driveway opposite. Couldn't remember their names, we'd barely spoken, our infrequent contact being centered around their huge and not-smart dog that sometimes escaped and went haring up and down the street, barking a huge great booming bark, as if trying to summon the dead from centuries past. Their drive was long and overhung with trees, Tesla and Nissan parked neatly at the end. I went to the door and rang the bell. After a few minutes, I rang it again.

As I was walking away, I heard something. Faint, way in back of the house. A dog. That enormous bark, muffled.

I went back to the door and peered through the big glass panel on one side. Tidy hallway, a couple of lights on. Door at the far end, probably gave entry to the kitchen. The dog had not come running through to bark at the front door, which implied he was in some other room without access to the run of the house.

MICHAEL MARSHALL SMITH

I've never been a dog person but my understanding is—especially with a hound that large and neurotic—you don't leave them for long periods. So why was it alone in there now?

I wasn't going to try every damned house. I was 99% sure that I was letting a bunch of coincidences seem more than it was. There was a simpler way of bursting this bubble, and more effective. Plus it would meet a need that was getting stronger by the minute.

IT PROBABLY DOESN'T say a lot for my quality of life that my most frequent trips out of the house are to the 7-Eleven, but bottom line is it stocks most of the things I need on the day-to-day. Beer for the evening. Something quick and lazy for lunch sometimes. Ours actually has organic milk. Their coffee is dire but it doesn't stop me drinking it from time to time. It also has the benefit of being only a four-minute drive from the house, or a half-hour round trip on foot if I'm feeling virtuous.

I was not feeling virtuous. I fetched the car keys and set off. I did not see anybody on the way down the street but I was, in a nervy way, becoming accustomed to that. What felt stranger was getting to

TIME OUT

Borland Street at the bottom. It's no wider than our street but is a main thoroughfare across the upper west side, one of only two routes that connect the University to downtown and the freeways. There's a steady stream of traffic along it, so much so that usually I would do a quick left then right before the bottom of our street in order to take advantage of the four-way stop at the next intersection along.

I didn't do that now. I didn't need to. There were no cars going in either direction. I waited for a minute. Nothing.

I had never encountered this before, ever.

I turned right. The road curves past two churches, a school and a bunch of houses. Everything looked normal except for the continued lack of moving cars and pedestrians. I drove slowly, glancing down each side street I passed. Everything motionless.

Eventually I took the left I'd been aiming for and pulled into the convenience store's lot. There were only two vehicles parked, one a white SUV, the other a battered once-green pickup. The 7-Eleven sees steady business from locals but especially the student community, as it's the nearest store to the campus and there's no alternative for anybody on the upper west side. There's a laundromat there too—Surf City Suds—which gets heavy use from the same demographic. I wasn't sure I'd ever seen fewer than a half-dozen cars in the lot, even on late-night cigarette missions.

I parked and went to look through the windows of the laundromat. Nobody inside. The door was locked. Maybe people didn't wash their clothes the day after Christmas.

I headed to the 7-Eleven. I pushed the door. This one opened. The lights were on and the interior looked as it always did. A bank of refrigerators along the back holding beer and juices, milk and iced coffee drinks, the Rosé that Leela likes once in a while. A couple of aisles offering the key food groups of student and stoner sustenance—instant ramen, potato chips, candy, cans of tuna, other very basic provisions. Another fridge on the left with pre-made sandwiches and salads in plastic containers.

Before that, the register. To one side, a small bank of rollers under hot lights held taquitos and franks, endlessly turning, keeping warm. There were a few items on there, not many. Behind the counter, the racks of what I'd come for. Cigarettes.

But no one to sell them to me. 'Hello?' I said. No response.

I went back to the door and stuck my head out. Some of the slackers who work the register will go have a smoke outside if the store is empty. No sign.

TIME OUT

They don't stray far, and I'd've seen them when I arrived. But I was being methodical.

Back inside I called out again. Then wandered to the back corner, where there's a small office. The door was slightly ajar. It seemed unlikely the clerk would retreat in there without being able to see the store—even though every time you open the exterior door it makes a loud pinging sound—but I knocked on it anyway.

No response. I nudged it wider with my foot. The space beyond was as flamboyantly untidy as when I'd glimpsed it before: that'd always been late at night, when strictures like the "This Door To Be Closed At All Times" sign was ignored. There was nobody in there. I pulled the door back the way it had been.

Waited in the main area for ten minutes. Left.

6

FORTY MINUTES LATER I was downtown, parked on the main street. Plenty of spaces. Curious in itself—usually you can whistle for a street spot and instead have to use the two-story lot around the corner—and consistent both with the 7-Eleven's parking lot and something else I'd since realized about my time in it.

Getting to Pacific Avenue had taken less than ten minutes. I'd spent the next half-hour walking up the street one way, all the way to the end of the shopping area (only four blocks, it's not a big town) and then back. I was now reviewing the information this had provided. And standing in the middle of the road.

I was there because there was absolutely nobody around, and hadn't been the entire time. Not a single person. There had been no traffic on the roads en route, even when I crossed Mission, which is a section of Highway 1 itself and *always* busy.

MICHAEL MARSHALL SMITH

All the stores were locked, though it was now mid-day. As I'd walked down and then back up the street, an idea occurred to me. That this was a dream. It took less than an instant to dispel. It wasn't. Soon as you ask yourself the question—I've had a few semi-lucid dreams in the past—the answer is self-evident.

This led quickly to another idea.

That I was dead.

Ludicrous idea, but oddly harder to dispel. Having never been dead before I didn't know how you'd tell. As someone who makes shit up for a living (I should have explained before, I'm a pretty unsuccessful television writer) I could make the narrative pieces fall into place quickly. Last night I fell asleep kinda-drunk while playing Legos. Woke to find nobody around. Decided to go check on people, make nice with Leela. Or maybe start a fight. Tripped on the stairs, fell, broke my neck. Or else my wife waited until I'd come to bed and gone to sleep, then smothered me with a pillow. Different kind of show, but you could make it work.

Neither was remotely credible.

While Leela and I may fight occasionally we're a long road from the "smothering him in his sleep" point. And I don't start arguments—or continue them—for the sake of it. I had been nowhere near

TIME OUT

falling-down drunk. I'd cleaned up the kitchen after waking. Of course you could go down a rabbit hole of arguing that I merely *imagined* I'd done this, but that way lay madness. I felt exactly as I should, down to the dusty feeling of a mild hangover, and I was beginning to *really* want a cigarette.

Would those be likely if I was dead?

It was impossible to know. It seemed likely there'd be *some* way of telling, however, some noticeable difference in the way I felt in myself and in my body. There was none. I couldn't *prove* I was alive but for now I was going to assume so until presented with strong evidence to the contrary. I put the question aside.

So what I was turning over in my mind—as I stood in the middle of the street, relishing the wrongness while hoping that it wouldn't be long before someone honked at me, or a cop strode over to ask what the fuck I thought I was doing—were the locked doors up and down all the stores. The laundromat by 7-Eleven had also been locked, the lot almost empty—like the parking spaces along this street. The downtown stores didn't give me much to work on. Most shut by seven p.m. and almost none opened before ten a.m. The 7-Eleven was open twenty-four hours and so didn't help either.

Surf City Suds stayed open until one a.m., however, and opened again five hours later. That gave me a time frame. Whatever happened must have occurred in that slot.

Somewhere between one a.m. and six a.m., everybody had disappeared.

NO CAR HONKED. I did not look up to see a cop or anybody else vocally wondering what the hell I was doing in the middle of the street. I went back to the car and drove around for an hour. Up and down side streets. Over the river into mid-town. To the main beach and the foot of the wharf—where people are *always* to be found, walking up and down, checking out the sea lions, especially on holidays. It's a tourist town.

Nobody, anywhere.

On the way home I stopped again at 7-Eleven. I got some Organic 2% milk from the fridge plus a six-pack of Anchor Steam. Took it up to the counter. Waited a while.

Then—feeling very strange indeed—walked around the side and helped myself to a pack of cigarettes.

I left thirty bucks next to the register.

7

AT FIVE O'CLOCK I got a beer from the fridge and took it out on the deck. It was a little early for this. Usually Leela and I defined 5:30 p.m. as cocktail hour and were strict about it. It had long been our custom to head outside with a drink at that time, and the conversations we had not only resolved most of the difficulties we'd encountered in our lives but also led to some of our boldest decisions—including moving to Santa Cruz.

I sat in my customary chair, took a sip of beer and lit a cigarette, feeling the customary cessation of guilt at being allowed to do it, as it was now 5:01 p.m. I smoked it while looking down over my usual view of the garden, watching a variety of local birds taking hectic advantage of the feeder that hangs from the tree at the end of the deck. That felt normal too.

Nothing else did. The other chair was empty. That happened from time to time if Leela went out with friends or was cooking, but there's a difference if you don't know where the hell your wife is. Or daughter. Or anybody else at all.

The phone system was still down. Internet too. Nobody had walked past the house in the several hours I'd spent watching. None of the cars had moved. I had seen several birds and a number of squirrels. Nothing else. The power still worked. My beer was cold. So was the next one. I was not going to go over quota—long experimentation has shown I can drink four not-too-strong beers and a small glass of red wine and get up the next morning as if nothing happened—but I was sure as hell going to walk right up to the line and stand on it.

I do not, incidentally, have a drinking problem, whatever the fuck-up on Christmas Day may imply. I simply like my beers at the end of the day. Kind of a ritual. In the general run of things Leela is as likely to find herself the other side of sober, not least because she doesn't have as mathematical a system for sticking to quota. It doesn't happen with either of us often. We have a child. Somewhere.

I was missing Leela—not least as I only ever sat in this spot, looking out over the pool, when chatting with her. During the afternoon the lack of Emily had moved into first place, however. I don't think people without kids realize how much their arrival shifts your gears around, pushing your own self from the center of creation. Maybe some people feel that way about their pets, in which case, fair enough. Emily's presence in my life had caused me to make decisions (and decline to make others) that established her as one of my prime directives. Possibly the core one. And now I had no idea where on earth she was.

I was aware of the hoppy taste of the beer, and the texture of the air—one that three years in town had taught me presaged overnight sea fog—and the vague feeling that I needed to pee when I went in to get the third beer. None of these details felt consistent with the idea of being dead. I'd returned to the question several times over the course of the afternoon and each time felt satisfied with the holding conclusion that it wasn't the case. I'd only even reconsidered it because I literally didn't know what else to think.

I had a plan, of sorts. Though I hadn't exactly grid-searched the place, my drive after visiting downtown earlier suggested that whatever this situation was, it obtained over the whole of what I thought of as "town". I'd come back along a short stretch of Highway 1 and seen no other cars either on it or even at the always-busy junction with Highway 17. The fact I'd encountered nobody driving into Santa Cruz ominously suggested this wasn't restricted to this town: lots of people commute from over the hill in Silicon Valley and even more come up Highway 1 from the poorer neighborhoods down around Watsonville. I'd seen no sign of crashed cars or vehicles off the side of the road, which perhaps suggested that whatever changed the situation from the way it was before, to how it was now, couldn't have been instantaneous. Unless the cars then in movement had vanished too, which seemed a stretch. Though who knew what constituted a "stretch" in these conditions?

My intention was to wait it out for the evening. Hope my family miraculously re-appeared for dinner, or at least that phones and the Internet started working again. If not I'd go to bed in the probably equally vain hope that being asleep for a while would somehow reset everything. I hadn't seriously reconsidered the idea that this was all a fucking dream—but again, who knew?

If not, I had most of a tank of gas. I could be down in Monterey in forty minutes, or up in San Francisco in an hour and a half, with enough gas to get home again. In some ways the latter made more sense. Going to a much larger conurbation would be more conclusive. On the other hand it

TIME OUT

would involve nearly three times the time (and gas) commitment.

And also...the idea of leaving home at all was not appealing. It felt safe here. Or safer, anyway. And I wanted to be home when Emily got back. Leela too. Assuming they ever did.

I shook that thought away and finished my beers. Drank my allowed glass of red at the kitchen counter, picking at yesterday's leftovers. Considered going for a walk, knocking on a few doors. Decided I did not feel like it.

Instead I plugged in my phone, and Leela's, and my laptop, to charge fully in case the power stopped at some point. I turned on the television in the family room—directly underneath our bedroom—and tuned the cable box to CNN. The screen was blank and the channel was silent. I turned the volume up to where a point that, should it come on during the rest of the evening, or the night, I'd immediately hear it. I'm not sure why I'd decided that CNN would be the first to come back, if anybody did. I guess you have to pick something.

It was only seven thirty. I tried to read for a while, then fetched the laptop and set it up on the kitchen table and did some work. It was not clear to me whether this was purely out of habit or a gesture of hope. It passed the time.

I passed a little more time later sitting in darkness in the living room, watching the road outside. Nothing changed, and nobody returned.

Before I went to bed I went up to Emily's room and said goodnight in the emptiness.

8

WHEN I WOKE, everything was the same. I was somewhat prepared for this, having woken briefly at a little after two a.m., and again before four, to discover I was still in bed alone and there was no sound from the television in the room below. It felt different getting out of bed to it, however, as though that change in circumstance made it more real. I'd had enough sleep to establish that "waking" could be ticked off a list of potential solutions.

I drank a lot of coffee, glad I'd thought to pick up milk in the 7-Eleven. I showered—the water still worked too—and dressed. Then I drove to Monterey, having decided during a period of wakefulness that this would be plenty far enough.

I pulled out of the drive at 8:15. Highway 1 remained empty and by 8:30 I'd passed the smaller ancillary towns of Aptos and Freedom and was arcing around the bay, where there's little but agricultural land on either side. I considered pulling over at Moss Landing, a traditional family coffee stop, but there were no cars in the lot and no signs of life. I kept going. There was nobody working in the fields. No machinery in movement. Twenty minutes later I passed Seaside, normally a rush of cars entering or leaving the freeway. Even though I slowed the car to a halt and sat there in the fast lane for five minutes, I saw no one.

Not long after that I took the exit to head into downtown Monterey. It was immediately clear what the conditions were but I kept going, as if on autopilot, until I reached Cannery Row.

There were only a handful of other vehicles parked on the street. The stores, restaurants, tourist shops and Starbucks were all empty and locked. The hotel was too, consistent with the event having happened after one a.m., which a sign to the side of the doors cited as the time after which residents would need a key card to gain entry. Presumably if I'd had one I could have got in and poked around, but I did not. At the end of the street I tried the doors to the world-famous aquarium, which I knew from experience was hellishly busy on the holidays. Locked, and empty inside, from what I could see through the big glass doors. A few ceiling lights were on. No other sign of life. I was past

TIME OUT

the point where illuminated lightbulbs qualified as such.

As I walked back to the car muscle memory made me glance toward the Fish Hopper restaurant, as I was in the habit of buying a pint of their clam chowder to take home whenever we passed through. I wandered along the boardwalk toward it. Tugged fruitlessly at the door, and suddenly found myself shouting at it. I guess because it was a place we'd been to many times, and it being so resolutely closed. The shouting achieved nothing.

I backed away, shaking, taken aback by the outburst of emotion. Walked over to the railing to calm down. As I stood there smoking and looking confusedly out over the bay—a pair of sea otters were playing in the swell thirty yards away, confirming yet again that whatever had taken place had not affected local wildlife—I realized something else.

No chemtrails.

The sky was wide and open and blue, the specific shade it affects when late summer's turning into autumn. No sign of planes. Now I thought about it, trying not to panic, I was pretty sure I'd heard none in the last twenty-four hours. Santa Cruz is on a flightpath to SFO, San Francisco's busy airport. Anything coming from LAX or Burbank or San Diego or any number of smaller regional airports goes right over our house, usually a couple of times an hour—thankfully high enough not to come with noise.

If I'd consciously noticed this before, I would have realized the trip to Monterey was pointless. Doubtless the same was true north of Santa Cruz too. Whatever this situation was, it extended further than it made any sense to drive.

WHEN I GOT back to Borland Street I continued past our street and on to the 7-Eleven, grimly aware that even post-apocalypse—or whatever the fuck this was—it was remaining my key destination. The problem with drinking four beers a night rather than three is a six-pack doesn't last two nights. This is one of the many cycles of life I am powerless to affect. The parking lot hadn't changed. Same two vehicles. Laundromat locked and empty.

My thirty bucks was still by the register. The same taquitos and franks—now looking quite dark and dry—were still gently revolving on the rollers. After a moment's thought I got a container, lifted the food off, and put them in it. Not to take home (though honestly, the steak and cheese taquitos aren't bad) but out of a vague concern that if they

TIME OUT

spent much longer going round and round they might catch fire.

I put them to one side and went to the fridge. Decided I might as well get a twelve-pack (which I did once in a while, because it's divisible by four, though won't fit in the fridge), and picked up a bottle of red wine in passing. At the counter I realized I didn't have enough cash. I dutifully went outside to the ATM in the wall of Surf City Suds, to discover it wasn't working. Of course. It doubtless depended on some kind of Internet feed.

I went back into 7-Eleven and behind the counter and prepared to figure out how to ring up the sale on the register so I could pay for it with my phone...before realizing this would require the Internet too. So *now* what did I do?

You take the fucking beer anyway.

The thought dropped into my head in Leela's voice. Or, more accurately, in a tone similar to the one she'd used when explaining that I was an asshole on Christmas Day. It landed with a deep and resonant thud, because it was kind of a game-changer.

There was nothing to stop me just taking the goddamned beer. Literally nothing.

I picked up yesterday's cash from the counter.

I could take anything I wanted. Any drink. *All* the drinks. The food, for what it was worth.

Anything I wanted in the office. If I so desired, I realized with a dark kind of giddiness, I could get back in the car and drive downtown and find a brick and smash the window of any store down there and empty it of contents.

For a moment I was lost in this idea.

Then I found paper and a pen and wrote down the total for the goods I was taking (adding yesterday's beer and cigarettes and milk) and my phone number.

I left it by the register and drove home.

9

I SPENT THE afternoon working. Yeah, I know. Until I had reason to accept this situation was permanent, however, there was no reason not to. No other obvious activity to undertake. The kitchen couldn't get any tidier. Work has always been my go-to when the world is trying my patience through being inexplicable, disappointing, or scary. All of the above were currently true.

I worked at the table in the living room, keeping half an eye on the street. Nothing changed. I kept glancing up every ten minutes nonetheless, on the lookout for something in particular. Quite soon into the first, hard COVID lockdown, I'd seen a coyote sitting on our lawn in broad daylight. In the following days I'd seen it—or another similar—ambling down the street. Wildlife is highly-attuned to the density of humans in their environment. I wasn't especially concerned about the presence of coyotes (you see them up in the woods from time to time, and can generally frighten them off with a shout or lunge, if they don't lope away as soon as they catch sight of you) but seeing one might provide evidence for the question of whether this was a long death dream, on the grounds that whoever was in charge of an afterlife would be unlikely to have provided that baroque detail.

At least, that had been my first thought.

After a while I'd brought myself around to the opposite conclusion, that this might be *exactly* the kind of detail that would be included—as the memory had come out of my own head. I had now been round and round on the subject to the point that I had absolutely no idea what I thought, but it was something to do. Pretty much my entire plan right now boiled down to finding something to do until the situation changed.

Then I thought: *Dog.*

When I'd rung on the door of the house opposite yesterday, there'd been a dog in there. It was, as I've said, a dumb dog. And I am a cat person. Emily had proved allergic to cats (to her huge disappointment), otherwise we'd have at least one. But I am in favor of animals in general and would not want one to be in discomfort. If there was a dog in the house over the street, and my guestimate over the approximate time of "the event"

TIME OUT

was correct, it had been alone for over thirty-six hours. Without food.

That wasn't okay.

I finished my coffee with a cigarette on the deck—having gotten past viewing daytime smoking as a betrayal of absent family—and set off across the street.

I RANG THE doorbell. Stood close to the door, head cocked. Didn't hear any barking. I rang again, and waited. Nothing.

I didn't know what dogs ate but assumed that as dog-owners the residents would have a stock on hand, probably in a bag with a picture of a dog on it. I'd figure it out. The lack of barking was throwing me, though. A dog in a house, abandoned, is a straightforward call to action. Without barking it was harder to rationalize my next move—i.e. breaking in.

I turned the door handle. It was locked. One of the householders doubtless did the same as me before retiring each night, checked all entrance points. The upper west side is a safe neighborhood but nobody takes risks like that anymore. I'd been known to forget our back door, however. That would be my best bet.

The house occupied almost all of the plot's width but on the left side there was a six-foot-wide wooden fence with a door in it. This door was locked too. The fence was about six feet high. Climbable. Just about. I squared up to it.

Even when you're pretty sure you're going to remain unobserved, it feels weird breaking into someone else's yard. For me, anyway, though I'd long been aware that for some, it did not. I'd been most forcefully struck by this one night in a hotel in London, years ago, looking out the window in the small and jetlagged hours to see a man sauntering along, trying car doors. One had been left unlocked and he was in and out in five seconds, emerging with something in his hand, which he took with him as he walked quickly but calmly away. By the time I'd registered what had happened it was too late to do anything about it.

I wondered if the world I lived in now was the one he inhabited all the time. A world in which other people effectively didn't exist, and it was all about him. I even considered for a moment whether this might be literally true—that in fact the world was exactly as it had always been, and I simply couldn't see anybody.

I decided this was too big an idea to deal with right now, and likely unverifiable, and anyway, I was here about the dog.

TIME OUT

But not wholly confident about the fence. Regular walking and irregular runs have kept me somewhat fit. I do sets of press-ups when I remember and go through periodic phases of visiting a gym. I am, however, demonstrably not nineteen, and there are times when my back and shoulders sternly remind me of this fact—notably my back, which has a tendency to go into minor spasm if I'm too cavalier with it. Such are the perils of the mid-forties, especially for people who spend too much time in the same position, hunched over a laptop.

I looked around for a box or large flowerpot or whatever to stand on. No luck. I could simply not-do this, of course. It was coming up for beer time. This wasn't my problem. I didn't even like the dog.

But I guess for most of us there's always someone watching, even if it's only yourself.

IT TOOK THREE attempts. None were elegant. My shoes didn't have much grip and the strength I'd retained in my upper arms wasn't optimized toward damn-fool activities like scaling a vertical wooden fence. On the first two tries I was punking it, too, protecting my back like an old person.

The third attempt finally saw me scrabbling up to a precarious position astride the fence. I felt very heavy up there. Not fat—I'm not—but really fucking *heavy*, as if the planet was keen that I rejoin it immediately, turning up the gravity just for me.

I managed to vault my leg over fairly smoothly and dropped down the other side clumsily but in one piece—feeling breathless, disconcerted, but slightly brave. Then I headed quickly down the side of the house. There was a window halfway along. A kitchen beyond. Tidier than the default state of ours (most people's are) and empty of people. Unsurprising not merely because of overall conditions, but because I'd not been quiet during my journey over the fence. Anybody inside would have come out to find out what the hell was going on. A second window showed a dining area connected to the kitchen, and then I was around the back of the house.

The yard, as with a lot of the dwellings in our neighborhood, was larger than you'd have guessed from the road. The area used to be a hilltop farm and when it was broken up for development the plots were sized generously. There was no pool and they'd gone with a large, simple rectangle of grass, but I guess if you have a huge dumb dog it needs somewhere to run around.

TIME OUT

The first half of the house's back extent was mainly glass. The kitchen/diner. The other half looked like a family room or something similar, also largely glass. Huge great television, its back to the garden, which isn't how I would have done it. Bookcase full of DVDs, a retro touch (I'd offloaded ours in a thrift store in the mountains two years back) and a smaller one with some actual books. Two couches and a couple of chairs. And—

Fuck.

I didn't see it right away because of the unit holding up the TV. Beyond that, in the side wall, a sliding door, largely glass. The dog was lying on the floor in front of it. I moved to the side to get a better view. Then wished I hadn't. Really wished I hadn't.

Maybe hunger. In a way, I hoped so. Because the alternative was loneliness.

There was a scattering of objects on the floor. A few books, two small vases. All, I suspected, had been knocked off as the dog had gone round and round the room. Perhaps slowly at first, but then faster and faster. Unable to comprehend his situation or why he was alone. Why his pack had abandoned him.

Then the door. Maybe this was the way the dog was normally let out of the house into the yard. Or perhaps there was a tiny gap at the bottom, letting odors in from the outside, something to remind the animal that's how he normally left the house, into the external part of his domain—the part where his humans could be found waiting to play, to throw him something to fetch or just pet him on the head and tell him he was a good boy.

He'd tried to get out there. Tried hard. The evidence was in a dried red-brown mess all over the lower part of the glass panel, and in what looked like splatters from his paws, higher up, as he had scrambled at it. But mainly the mess down below, a thick mass of blood and fur, from where the dog seemed to have run into the door many, many times, throwing his skull at it like a battering ram, frantically trying to get out.

All I could do was hope he'd caused enough damage to his head to have lost the ability to think and feel before he died.

10

FORTY MINUTES LATER I was outside Diamond Hardware, part of the short strip mall that adjoins the big Safeway on the lower west side. The lot was almost empty, another low-level reminder of the situation, one I noticed despite having no need to be reminded. I assumed my mind would accept this as business as usual at some point but I was in no hurry. Accepting it would likely not make anything worse, but it wouldn't make it better.

I parked in front of the hardware store and opened the trunk. A few cardboard boxes from the garage—they'd been full of generic family crap but I'd emptied it out onto the floor—a spade, and a selection of screwdrivers. I left the boxes by the car on the grounds that unless the other objects achieved their purpose there was no point carrying the boxes over. I did bring one further thing from the passenger seat.

The store doors were big and glass and, naturally, locked. Very firm, too, no sign of give. I fiddled about at the joins with a screwdriver but could see no way of opening them. Hardly a surprise. There were a few large BBQ grills arrayed to either side, but they'd been tightly chained to the structure to stop people stealing them in the night. Again, as I'd expected.

So it was the spade or nothing.

I propped it against the door and put on the other thing I'd brought from the car—Emily's noise-canceling headphones, a big-ticket gift from her last birthday. They had looked comically large on her small and happy head, and the memory made me feel grim. It had felt odd and sad getting them from her room, more odd even than the prospect of breaking into the hardware store, a place I'd been to many times. Enough to know that the guy who owned the franchise had a bunch of pets, and thus, unlike a lot of such places, stocked the kind of stuff I was looking for.

I grabbed the spade and stood to the side of the left-hand door, shoving one of the grills aside to give me room. This, I hoped, would yield some protection when the glass doors broke. I did not want some large shard slicing down to hack a large chunk off me. Or, worse, going straight down through my head. The headphones were to protect

TIME OUT

my ears against the alarm, which I'd be standing directly underneath.

I think things through. Almost always.

I got close to the wall, braced myself, closed my eyes, gently swung the spade in an arc so that the metal end would smack the door in the middle of the sheet of glass. Adjusted the position of my feet by a couple of inches. Gathered myself, issuing a stern reminder *not* to do it with all my strength, as that'd be as likely to screw up my back as scrambling over a neighbor's fence. Then swung the spade head at the door. Very hard.

Of course it didn't fucking break.

Not that time, nor the five subsequent tries. All they achieved was making my wrists hurt. I threw the spade down after the last attempt, panting, feeling dumb and angry, the same spastic fury building inside that had caused me to shout at the locked door of the Fish Hopper down in Monterey.

Of course the doors were tough, otherwise the place would be robbed every night. You MORON.

This was...suddenly, it all felt too much.

Way too fucking much. I was scared and panicking and strung out from being alone and nothing making sense. I stomped back to the car, leaving the spade where it was. It was useless. Fuck that spade. Left the boxes on the ground too.

Kicked up the engine, ready to drive the fuck home, and you know what? Maybe *not* stick to quota tonight. Who cared?

Then I found myself putting the car in Drive instead of Reverse. I didn't slam my foot down, just eased it as if I was pulling away from traffic lights. I angled the car as it started to move forward and bumped up over the curb, so it was the front right corner of the vehicle that hit the hardware store's doors.

The left door of the store shattered.

Simply, and without much mess. The store alarm went off, a more anemic sound than I'd been fearing. Presumably it reported back to a monitoring center, so on-site noise was kept to a sane level. I smiled at the broken door through my windshield, which had taken no damage whatsoever.

'Ha,' I said. 'Fuck you, door.'

I got out. Almost no damage to the front of the car—a short scratch in the paintwork. Evidently the gods were with me on this mission. I grabbed the cardboard boxes and went into the store.

FIFTEEN MINUTES LATER I'd gathered everything I'd come for. Food for both dogs and cats.

TIME OUT

Two short step ladders—light enough that I'd be able to swing one over onto the other side of any scalable fence, and descend less chaotically than I had at our neighbor's. A range of tools including crow bars, a battery-driven drill and a small portable circular saw.

I worked out the total, wrote it down on a piece of their stationery, added my number, wondering how long I was going to keep doing this. Then wrote my number on a second sheet of paper too and grabbed sellotape.

When I'd carried all the stuff and our spade to the car I went back to stick the second sheet to the non-broken side of the doors. The alarm had continued for the duration but for short intervals of silence every five minutes, the standard ruse to stop people becoming so accustomed to a sound they stop considering whether they should do anything about it. Assuming it kept this up, it was as good a way as I could think of to alert anyone within hearing distance that there was another human abroad.

I stuck the sign up without great optimism. It was simply another idea. Another thing to do. I could picture myself coming back here in a week and seeing the sign still there, and realized that at some level I was getting used to the idea that I'd become the guy in that story *I Am Legend*. Except without the cool vampires. Without anybody at all, in fact.

I drove away, trying to view the tinny ringing of the alarm as a clarion call of triumph in the first part of my mission. It worked, kind of, though mainly it just sounded lonely.

I WAS VERY ready for a beer when I got home. Before I'd registered what was happening, I'd suddenly had three. Irritated with myself, I decided I wasn't embarking on my mission tonight. Clambering over fences and breaking into houses in search of animals that needed feeding was a good idea. For them, and also for me—or else I was going to wind up like Dumb Dog across the road, pacing around the house in faster and faster circles until something snapped in my brain. Doing it a little drunk was a *bad* idea, though. If I fell, or fucked up using a tool and gashed myself, there was no 911 to call. I had no desire to end my days lying on my back unable to move, or bleeding out.

I hadn't tried the phone since the morning. I did so as I fetched my last beer. Nothing had changed there or on the laptop. I drank the beer, watching a pair of doves making use of the birdfeeder. I did not

TIME OUT

bother eating any leftovers. I was bored of them. I didn't do any work either. I was bored of that too.

And I was tired. Dog tired. There was no one around to care about the pun. At some point during the evening a bubble burst. The nervous tension I'd been churning through since I'd established Leela and Emily weren't in the house began to dissipate. Once that started it went fast, leaving me quiet and empty and still. It'd been quite a while and there's a limit to how long you can sustain fight-or-flight. Maybe what happened to the dog contributed, too, combined with the fact that I had, in full view of the entire world, broken into a hardware store and taken what I wanted and brought it home, with zero consequence.

I was alone.

The only thing I could do was pass the time.

11

I WAS UP early next morning, ready to go. During periods of wakefulness in the night I'd come up with a system.

I'd mentally marked off an initial catchment zone, bounded at the top by the woods and the bottom by Borland. An area extending south of our street as far as the section where a minor gulley forms a natural boundary within the residential area, and north extending to the school, about half the distance to 7-Eleven.

That would be… I didn't know how many houses. You couldn't even describe it in blocks, as there's not much of a grid pattern on the upper west side. Quite a lot. Certainly enough to start with. I thought it made sense to do this rather than simply setting off in one direction and keeping going. I also decided it'd be prudent to do a first pass, attempting to establish by sight and sound from outside whether there were animals within each house, rather than charging into the first one. Gaining entry to a property would take a while unless I smashed my way in, which I wasn't intending to do out of vestigial respect for other people's property, along with the fact that any animals within would then be let loose. There was no point gaining access via *any* means if there was nothing in there to feed—and the time wasted might prevent me getting to other, animal-housing buildings in time.

It'd now been over forty-eight hours. Dumb Dog (the name felt disrespectful but had stuck in my head) might have been unusually neurotic but even the calmest of cats would be extremely hungry by this point. I wouldn't take tools or food on first reconnaissance. I'd come back and collect them when I knew where they were required. I was however going to take rolls of duct tape, in the three colors—white, blue and black—I'd been able to unearth from drawers in the garage. White for "Cat present"; Blue for "Dog present"; Black for "No sign of pets".

I didn't have a color for parakeets or pythons or anything else but I figured I'd deal with that problem if it came to it, not least because I didn't have food for them either.

The first pass took five hours.

I found nothing.

TIME OUT

AS I THOUGHT it over, while picking distractedly over bits of very dry turkey for a late lunch, I knew this made no sense.

Some of the neighbors *definitely* had animals. I'd seen a few faces out walking dogs regularly enough that they had to be very local (annoyingly, I couldn't remember seeing any of them going into a particular house). I'd seen a cat in the neighborhood at least once a day. A big ginger male most often, sometimes a more slender one I suspected was an Abyssinian, another that was Standard Issue Cat. Others, from time to time. A cat's territory can be large, however, especially younger males, so it was *slightly* credible all the ones I'd seen in the past had strayed into the street from outside the boundaries I'd set.

Possible, yes, but *likely*?

And I wondered: had I even *seen* a cat in the last couple days? I didn't think so. In fact, I was sure of it. I like cats. I notice them. I will go up and stroke one if they'll let me, or at least address it verbally in a respectful way. My mother always does this and I picked up the habit. I wondered briefly and not for the first time if she and my dad were okay, or if they'd vanished too. I shelved the thought, again.

Nothing I could do to find out, short of driving all the way to Vermont.

I'd seen squirrels and birds in the last couple days but no cats. And in fact...had I actually seen a squirrel this morning? I didn't think so. Despite the neighborhood being rife with them.

I stopped trying to eat.

AT FIVE THIRTY I was on the deck. Tired, not only mentally this time. I hadn't carried my phone during the day so I didn't know how many steps I'd taken while crisscrossing the area but it'd been a *lot*. My feet hurt. By late afternoon, baffled, I'd strayed outside the zone in all directions except the woods.

I'd stood listening outside some houses two or three times, done complete circuits of every single property. Neither sight nor sound of a single pet. I'd even, before giving up, carefully broken into three dwellings at random, thinking if I found dead animals in there it might be a sign my idea had simply come to me too late. None yielded any sign of animal occupants either in person or via obvious accommodations to them like pet beds or bags of food.

TIME OUT

I wasn't going to break into every single house. I carefully re-closed the doors of the ones I'd been in, in case domestic animals were better at hiding than I was at finding. I hadn't seen a single squirrel all afternoon, either.

And the birdfeeder was deserted tonight.

12

I WAS STILL out on the deck two hours later. In the meantime I'd fetched a hoodie—Santa Cruz evenings get chilly after darkness falls—and a notepad. Usually when I'm writing I simply go for it. Get a vague structure in my head and start typing, fixing problems as I go, re-organizing or re-structuring as required, accepting that the second draft may need to turn the first on its head. It's my process, such as it is. Once in a while it fails me. I'll hit a roadblock. I've learned there's no point banging my head against it. You're in too deep with the typing by that point, can't see the wood for the trees. So I step back, grab a notepad and pen. Write out names and events. Draw connections between them. Sketch little faces, or landscapes, whatever comes out of my hand and the pen. Doodle. Think.

There's probably some scientific reason why this (generally) helps. Occupying the busy, shouty half of my brain with activity so the deep thinking bit can do its work in peace. The tactility of using a pen, instead of a keyboard. Whatever. It's a sufficiently well-established practice that Leela will sometimes, when she senses I'm struggling at my desk, gently suggest: 'Maybe you need to go to the pad?'

So that's what I was doing. Going to the pad.

THUS FAR IT'D produced some mildly attractive abstract doodles and a single word, in ornate, shaded capitals.

RAPTURE.

Not a description of my mental state. The religious thing. I only knew it as a term. I couldn't look up further information as I had no relevant books and the Internet was still absent—most likely, I now accepted, permanently so—but the gist as I recalled it was that God would at some point decide the experiment had gone on long enough and yank the good folks up to Heaven to hang out and feel smug, leaving sinners and wastrels behind. I didn't believe in God, but as I hadn't previously believed the rest of humankind could vanish overnight—leaving behind functioning delivery systems for electricity and running water—I was acknowledging the possibility that

TIME OUT

my previous belief system had not been sufficient to cater for every eventuality.

It would though seem harsh if I'd been the only human found wanting, surely. I'm not perfect, but come on. I knew for a fact that one of the younger clerks in Diamond Hardware bought vapes and sold them to teenagers, because I'd seen him doing precisely that when sitting outside the pub at the end of the strip mall, having a beer with Mark. Perhaps in celestial terms that counted only as a misdemeanor, rather than an actual "sin". Or maybe there was something I'd done that ranked as a very particular infringement of dealbreaker God rules. I couldn't think what it might be, what thing I could have done that *nobody* else in town might not also been guilty of at some point in their lives.

I'd also always guessed the Rapture would be an "event", much as I'd assumed what had taken place here in town was an "event". Today's observations undermined that. Yesterday morning there'd been at least one dog in the neighborhood, and plentiful squirrels. A hard day's search today had found no pets and I'd seen no squirrels all day. In the three hours I'd been out on the deck not a single bird had come to the feeder. Okay, it was now dark, but I didn't believe that was the issue. I'd heard no bird song during the afternoon. Things had changed, progressed, in the last forty-eight hours. This opened the door to the idea this was not an event after all, but a *process*.

What that meant…was what I'd been trying to figure out. Unsuccessfully. Eventually I put the pad down. I thought about eating but couldn't get the idea to gain traction. There wasn't much in the fridge as I'd been intending to go grocery shopping on Boxing Day. The leftovers were tired, and I think I was also resistant to the idea of finishing them for other reasons. Once I did, the last meal I'd shared with my family would be gone.

All of it would be gone.

13

AT SOME POINT after midnight I was out walking. Didn't have the phone so I didn't know the exact time. I didn't need to. I did have the bottle of wine, but was only sipping. Somewhat performatively. I was trying to feel free.

I didn't look like some kind of wino or weirdo because there was no one to see, right? Without judgers there is no judgement, if you choose to ignore your own. I didn't have to work anymore. There was no one there to chase me on the deadlines that seemed so pressing on Christmas Eve—had contributed, in fact, to me being an asshole to Emily the next day. Those pieces of work had no home. They could remain unfinished, fictional characters frozen in non-time, never finding out what happened next. All the hours and months and years that I'd spent pecking away in the word mines had turned out to be pointless. They'd paid the bills and given me a sense of purpose and once in a while, even a little satisfaction. But where had they all been pointing?

Nowhere, after all that.

Words could look after themselves, or fade quietly to silence. I was free of them. I was free to drink. Free to smoke when I wanted. Free not to care if I put on weight. A vague neurotic concern about my shape had plagued my entire adult life. I was fine, only a few pounds over what I might have considered ideal, but this had been maintained by often choosing not to eat what I wanted. There'd been no point to *that*, either, but now nobody was left to make me ludicrously ornate French dishes or indulgent sandwiches or rich sauces, unless I chose to do it myself.

I was free to think or say whatever I pleased. There was nothing unthinkable. Nobody to care or cancel me. Free to get up whenever I wanted, or not at all. There were no constraints upon my existence whatsoever except ones consistent with an intention to stay alive. Assuming the continued desire to remain so.

The thing about being absolutely free, though, is you don't feel free at all. Total freedom doesn't count. What counts are those moments when you feel *temporarily* free. When the meeting you'd been wearily dreading gets pushed at the last minute, and you've suddenly got an hour to yourself that

TIME OUT

you hadn't been anticipating. Or those few minutes in the early morning, before anybody else is up and you have to start dealing with emails or calls or errands. Half an hour over a solo coffee or beer in an airport, surrounded by strangers, none of whom expect anything of you, few of which are even truly aware that you exist. An hour at the end of the day with your wife out on the deck, talking about whatever comes into your heads, with something to eat already in the oven and nothing more to do except put it on a plate.

Brief moments when you're simply *there*, living, not worrying about the next thing or the last thing or having to meet anybody's expectations, including your own.

That forever, though? That isn't free.

It's uncomfortably like retirement. Or death.

I RAMBLED AROUND the neighborhood for an hour or so. There was a kind of purpose to this, as I'd noticed a few houses earlier with lights on, and wondered if a clearer glimpse into their interiors at night might enable me to spot an animal, a cautious cat perhaps, crept out of hiding to look for food under cover of quiet.

I didn't see any. I did revisit one of the houses I'd broken into that afternoon, however, which had the opposite effect. While shambling around their kitchen I noticed a low cupboard I hadn't spotted the first time. Inside were several neatly-stacked boxes of cat food, the top open and missing several cans. I couldn't find a bowl or litter tray but could be the animal had been trained to strict mealtimes and to shit outdoors on a schedule.

I looked around the house to no avail. Some evidence of fur on what must have been a favorite chair. No actual cat, however. They'd all gone, along with dogs and squirrels and birds and presumably the sea otters I'd seen in Monterey yesterday. Maybe the Rapture spaceship to Heaven had limited room and they'd returned to pick up the non-humans on a second trip. If Dumb Dog had waited a little longer, he could have gone with them.

Back in the house's kitchen I stood sifting through the silverware drawer. Forks, spoons, knives. A couple of elastic bands. An ice-cream scoop. The usual crap. All looked like artefacts from some other civilization. Things designed for a purpose. Now merely objects within another object.

It all felt extremely final.

→ ←

TIME OUT

PERHAPS BECAUSE OF that, the sense that today might be the last of all possible days, I found myself unable to go to bed when I got back to the house. Like when you're young and don't want to bail to bed on your birthday because that'd mean your special day was over. Kind of like that, anyway. But also not.

I sat on the floor in Emily's room. Looked at all the things on the walls and the books on her shelf, some of which I'd read to her, a few of them many times.

I hoped I'd been kind enough, fatherly enough. I'd been busy, preoccupied, some of the time. But not all of it. I remembered many days when we'd laughed together, played together, looked across at each other and simply smiled. We'd done that. Those things had happened. But had they happened *enough*? I'd always assumed there would be so much time. The leisure to make sure childhood shone in Emily's memory as the Good Old Days, a golden age to cleave to in memory through the long slog of adulthood.

But it had gone so fast. Gone in an instant. No way back.

After a while, noticing my cheeks were wet and deciding this wasn't serving me, I went downstairs. I still didn't want to go to bed though my mind was finally quietening and I stood a chance of sleeping before long. I wound up on the couch. My laptop was there so I established for the ten millionth time that the Internet remained off. I picked up Leela's phone next. No signal. Well, a signal but it wouldn't connect: a distinction that possibly meant something—I'd been over this a hundred times over the last couple of days, along with conundrums like the continuance of the power supply: my mind hadn't been dormant while traipsing around the neighborhood looking for animals that weren't there—but I had no idea what that meaning was.

I was about to drop the phone back on the cushion but then, because I was missing her, found myself keeping hold of it. Turning it over in my hands. Looking at signs of wear on its familiar silicon cover, in coral. Not a color I liked, at all. Mine is teal. I'd never needed reminding that my wife was not merely an extension of me—she was too distinctive, too much herself, and so there—but little things like that did it anyway. How could anybody like coral? She did. It was painful but also nice to be reminded of it right now. This very different person had been mine.

Or at least a part of my life, as I had been of hers.

I tapped the screen, knowing there'd be differences there too. The background on my phone is a subtle variegated tone so as to help the app icons stand out. Hers was a busy photograph of me and Emily, standing on the wharf, sweet but making it almost impossible to see the—

Except it wasn't.

The photo she'd had there for at least a year had gone, to be replaced with one just of Emily. I supposed it made sense—our daughter had changed physically in that period, and so, sure, replace it with one more recent. Felt strange that I wasn't in the picture too, though. It suddenly didn't feel like the phone I'd held many times, grabbing it to answer a call if she was up to her elbows in cooking, or else to sort out some technical snafu.

I clicked her email app. Not something I'd do normally—despite sharing a PIN, we respected each other's privacy—but she wasn't goddamned here, was she. She'd gone. Left me alone. I wanted to hear her voice. *See* her voice, in fact—we often communicated in writing, especially when I was away on business, quick texts, longer notes sometimes.

Her in-tray was the usual debacle. I use mine as a to-do list so it generally has fewer than five emails lurking there. Hers had over two thousand. Don't even start me.

I clicked on a couple. Client communications, and back and forths with friends. I glanced at a couple but not for long. Your partner's messages to other people always read oddly. It's a subtly different version of them to the one you know. Instead of being comforting, it felt distancing. I quit back out of the app.

On impulse I clicked on the next icon along, Notes. Quotidian stuff here, sorted by the last time they'd been edited. A grocery list—she'd been the one to run to the store for a few last food items on Christmas Eve. A note with ideas for gifts—some of which had come to fruition, as I knew from two days before. The one at the top was titled just with three periods.

I clicked on it. I read it.

Sat staring at the screen, absolutely motionless, feeling the hairs rise on the back of my neck.

I read it again, more slowly this time. It wasn't finished. I could tell even before it abruptly stopped in mid-sentence at the end of the third paragraph. Leela's prose is tight. She is, or was, a copywriter. Her prose is better than mine and she can crank it out, too. This wasn't a note or a piece of work. It was a draft of a message. Its tone was different to the ones I'd glanced at in her email app. It was a tone I recognized.

This message was to me.

It had been written, according to the date/time stamp, on Christmas Day evening, while I'd

TIME OUT

been crashed out on the couch. The first paragraph said she was writing because she needed to discuss something big, and felt it better to get the broad strokes down so I could read them before we talked face-to-face.

The second paragraph...

I could feel her gearing up to what she wanted to say. Knew that by the time the note made it to me, this part would have been more concise. Then she said, straight out, that she was inclined—though had not yet made a final decision—to leave me. Taking Emily with her. Arrangements had been made for a place for them to stay. A bag was packed.

The third paragraph said:

> I'm sure you'll guess immediately what's brought me to this point. No, it's not you being rude to Emily today, though that was a dick move: but I know you well enough to know that you'll wake up tomorrow realizing that, and try to make it better. But it's not that. I *know*, David. I know what happened between you and

It stopped there.

I closed the app, turned off the phone, put it on the couch. Gingerly, as if it contained radioactive material. The house was silent. There was no sound, anywhere in the world.

I felt sick.

I walked up to our bedroom as if stepping on clouds and went into the side part that functions as a dressing area. I opened the small door there that gives access to attic space. This is where our suitcases are kept. It was immediately apparent that one had been moved from the neat line in which they normally stood.

I lifted it. It was full.

I closed the door and went back down to the living room, where I found myself suddenly sitting on the floor.

I *did* know why she might have wanted to pack a bag.

But I hadn't known that *she* knew, too.

14

AT TEN THE next morning I was floating in the pool. I was naked. This wasn't a declaration of freedom from norms. I couldn't find my swimming shorts. I didn't swim often. The pool was Leela's domain, source of both exercise and recreation. In my twenties and thirties I'd dreamed of owning a house with a pool. An obvious indicator of semi-success, key indicator of lifestyle. Once it had come to pass, however, after a couple of years I somehow got out of the habit. That was probably metaphoric of something or other but right now I didn't have the heart to work out what.

The water was not warm and I wasn't enjoying the experience. It had simply seemed like something I could do. Leela's half-written note had gone round and round in my head and I hadn't been able to get to sleep. I tried until six a.m. then got woodenly out of bed. Noticed the pool as I stood drinking coffee in the kitchen, thought: why not? I actually enjoyed swimming, for short periods.

So why hadn't I done it more often? I was considering this question as I floated around. The best I'd come up with was a resistance to being told what to do. Leela often advocated swimming to me as a form of exercise. So often, in fact, it had set up a reaction in me. There was also the fact that if I got in the pool when Emily was there then she'd want me to stay in forever, well past the point where it'd stopped being fun for me.

Was I really *that* much of an asshole?

So much that well-meant advice from my wife caused a churlish reaction? Far *worse*, that the prospect of hanging with my child for a little longer than I'd anticipated was insupportable?

I could rationalize both. My working life had been characterized by being other people's bitch. Their deadlines, their bizarre or contradictory or unworkable notes, their unaccountable delays after requiring me to work seven-day weeks for months, often even their storylines. During office hours (which in my industry can mean 24/7 when the crunch is on) I had very little personal control. Perhaps this caused a knee-jerk reaction in my "leisure" hours, a tendency to think: No, this is *my* time—and I'm going to do what I want, when I fucking want to.

TIME OUT

Sure, maybe.

But...*sheesh*. Seriously?

Too late to change now. Too late also to do anything about what I'd discovered in the night except keep feeling a horrific churn of awfulness in the pit of my stomach. To have parted on those terms, not knowing that we *were* parting, or even what those terms had been...was too big to process right now. I would have given anything to have been able to make it right, or at least to have been able to explain—insofar as I could. To apologize.

But it was too late for that. For all of it.

Too late to have not been an asshole.

15

EVENTUALLY I SLEPT. Napped, at least. I woke on the couch, still naked apart from a wrapped towel, and thus cold, at three p.m.

I was hungry. I'd eaten barely anything yesterday and not much the day before. My brain didn't care much about this but my body was getting unhappy. Sure, I could flamboyantly ignore it because I was freaked out and confused and sad, but unless I was intending to starve myself to death (not a decision I was yet inclined to make) I might as well get on with it.

The leftovers were past the point of being remotely attractive but I still didn't want to scrape them into the trash. There were provisions in the cupboard but as Leela and I both cooked regularly, they were items like tins of tomatoes and chickpeas and chipotle in adobe. Ingredients instead of meals. There might come a day where I felt like standing in the kitchen diligently cooking up a homemade supper for one. Today was not that day. And I was running low on milk, and out of both beer and wine.

I watched out of the bedroom window as I dressed.

No squirrels. I hadn't seen or heard a single bird during my time in the pool. All gone.

I DROVE TO Safeway in silence. I like it that way. If there are other people in the car then you can chat, or else enjoy a (to me) pleasantly companionable silence. When by myself, I found it a good time to think. I liked the sound of the wheels on the road, ambient sounds through the window. This had caused family spats in the past. Leela didn't mind music, and Emily loved it. Usually the child won, and I suffered more-or-less in silence as the car was filled with the warbling of whichever corporate pop moppet was currently enjoying Emily's fealty. At the risk of appearing old, to me they all sounded as if they were all on the verge of lapsing into a coma and I found it genuinely difficult to tell the difference between them. On a road trip to Yosemite I'd hit the wall after a couple hours of this and turned the music off. This caused Leela, with her occasional tendency to go straight to the

TIME OUT

nukes, to muse aloud on how Emily would doubtless wind up leaving home as soon as she possibly could, as nobody could enjoy living in such a grey world of sepulchral silence. To be clear, Emily was right there in the car, listening.

I turned to stare at Leela. But she hadn't taken it back.

And Christ, maybe she'd been right. Maybe all this was a punishment for being selfish, too much inside my own head. For not understanding that however long the previous two hours of music had seemed, they would be nothing against the years and years of quiet after Emily left home.

For being an accidental asshole.

I would have given anything to be withstanding one of those singers now, but wasn't going to try to find one on the radio or my phone. I already knew, from hearing a snatch of one of Emily's most well-worn songs a few weeks back, when she wasn't with me, that the sound would be enough to wet my eyes with its terrible secrets about the passing of time: about what was true now, but would not always be. I wish I'd known that on that afternoon in the car. It was too late now. Too late for every—

Catching this thought, I told myself to shut the fuck up. Feeling sorry for myself the whole time would be really fucking annoying. My dad always said: *Don't whine, nobody cares. Just keep going.* He was right. Always, but most especially now.

Despite silence in the car and my window being half-down (I like real air regardless of the outside temperature, another thing that's led to spirited family discourse from time to time), it took far longer for me to notice than it should have. Past the point where I'd rolled into the lot. Past when I'd parked in a spot right in the vast middle, stopping at random, because I could. Past even the point when I'd got out.

My mind was on procedure. It seemed certain I'd have to drive into the doors of the grocery store, as with Diamond Hardware. This wasn't possible on the two corner entrances because they were positioned under concrete porticos with columns insufficiently wide-spread for the car to get through at the correct angle. That meant the middle doors. These were arranged in three pairs, grouped together on the wide front face of the store. The challenge was that a study metal railing protruded from the store between each pair. This made the middle set impossible to tackle and a tight angle to get to the other two. I'd been lucky to get away with little damage to the car last time. Sure, if I mashed it up then I could get myself another car by breaking into a house and finding keys to whatever vehicle was in their drive.

TIME OUT

But *this was my goddamned car.* In a world of nearly infinite things to help myself to, keeping hold of ones that were genuinely mine seemed important. For some reason.

I returned to my car. Drove to within twenty feet of the store, adjusting the angle. It was going to involve bumping up over the curb but that was okay. I didn't need much speed. Relentless pressure from the front of the vehicle would break the glass. I got out once more, to check the angle a final time.

And only *then* did I register it.

The Diamond Hardware alarm wasn't ringing.

I REALIZED BELATEDLY how very quiet it was in the lot.

I looked in the direction of the hardware store. The silence wasn't HOLY COW strange. The alarm ringing wasn't a long-term feature of the lot—which is why I hadn't clocked its absence immediately. But it was curious.

Fuck: don't tell me the power's gone off.

It had been fine when I left the house. Or at least when…actually, when? I made coffee half an hour before I left. Maybe a little longer. And the drive took ten minutes. The window could be as much as an hour. And it only required a split second for all the electricity to suddenly not be there anymore.

All at once the parts of me that thought they'd accommodated to the situation realized they hadn't. The end of power would make everything very much *not fucking okay*.

I glanced into Safeway and realized with huge relief that lights were lit in there. In the ceiling, and in the nearest bank of refrigerators. Thank god. So…what, then? The alarm broke? Or it was on a couple-hour maximum timer, to avoid pissing off local residents? It probably didn't matter but with my heart still beating from the prospect of a powerless post-not-quite-apocalypse, I found I needed to know.

I trotted over to Diamond Hardware, trying to figure out how I'd arrive at an answer to the question. My best guess—not great, I had no idea how these things worked—was to start by looking at… But then I stopped in my tracks.

At first I simply couldn't believe what I was seeing. I moved my head to the side, thinking maybe it was the way the light was catching it or… I didn't know. I took a few steps closer.

From there it was undeniable.

The glass door wasn't broken any more.

16

I WENT RIGHT up close. Reached out and touched it. The left door was back to being a single, smooth sheet of glass.

I took a couple steps back, utterly confused. Looked to either side. No glass on the floor, but the sheet of paper with my phone number was still stuck to the other side. I pressed my face right up against the door. The interior looked exactly as it had yesterday. I was caught between bewilderment, a small but growing sense of jubilation, and…something else.

I tentatively rapped a knuckle on the glass. 'Hello?'

My voice sounded odd to me. I'd spoken plenty over the last couple of days, in addition to the couple times I'd shouted at the world, or the Fish Hopper door. I talk to myself a fair amount, especially when I'm trying to figure things out. But it's different when you're trying to communicate with someone else.

No movement inside. I rapped again, harder. Kept doing it, at intervals, for five minutes. Looked up and down the walkway again. Walked out into the lot. Looked all around, turning three hundred and sixty degrees. No movement or people. Anywhere.

'Hello?' This time I said it loud. Then *very* loudly.

There was a faint echo as the sound hit the towering wall of Safeway and bounced back. Enough, for a split second, for me to think someone had returned the cry.

The belief was momentary but helped me place what my third feeling had been on discovering the reconstructed door. I'd got over the shock of it being back in place now. I'd banged my hand on it. It was simply a fact. The initial jubilation was muted now too, partly because the third feeling was…

Caution.

Extreme caution.

Did I *want* to see another human? Hell yeah. Though…with qualifications. Of course I wanted it to be Emily that I saw first, or Leela. Preferably both. But any person at *all* would suggest there was a chance this thing was different to what I'd assumed. I might not be alone. That would change everything. Not merely in practical terms, but in relation to what this all might mean. It would have

TIME OUT

been different however if I'd come upon someone while walking down the street. Or found a person in their house yesterday, sitting in undershorts guzzling stolen snacks and thinking they were alone in all the world. That'd make sense.

But *fixing the Diamond Hardware door?*

Where had they got the big sheet of glass? Was it even possible to single-handedly replace it? That glass would have been *heavy*. And then neatly sweeping away all the debris of the breakage? Why? My self-imposed (and now abandoned) mission of trying to look after pets was rational. Going around fixing broken doors? That was...that seemed *strange*.

I thought about shouting out again, decided I didn't want to. Decided that I didn't, in fact, want to be here at all.

When I got back to the car I checked the front right corner of the hood. The little scratch was there. I hadn't made up or dreamed smashing the door down. That happened.

I SPENT TWO hours in the living room with my pad and a lot of coffee and achieved nothing except more doodles, a headache, and a growing conviction that I was losing my mind. That started with the realization that leaving my phone number on the door of Diamond Hardware (and in 7-Eleven) had not been evidence of straight thinking. Sure, I could reassure myself I'd assumed if someone turned up to read it, this would be corelated with a general return to normal conditions, like the availability of the phone service, but the truth was I hadn't consciously considered the question. I'd simply forgotten the implications of the fact the fucking phone system was down. *How were they going to call?*

As my caffeine levels mounted I got to the point of considering whether I'd straight-up imagined smashing down one door of the hardware store, which is why it was in one piece today, then remembered I'd already looked for (and found) the scratch on the car. The fact I also had a number of bags of dog and cat food in the car—I went and checked twice—didn't reassure me as much as it should. Nor the fact that I had a clear memory of the Diamond Hardware logo on the sheet of paper still stuck to their door, which I could only have got from inside.

I re-considered the idea I'd had when preparing to vault over the fence into the opposite neighbor's garden yesterday. What if everybody *was* actually

TIME OUT

still here? What if normal life *was* still going on but I was unable to perceive it?

That'd explain how the door had been repaired. It'd explain why the power and other utilities still worked.

Though not why the Internet and phones were down. That didn't track. And I'd broken into the hardware store in broad daylight. Why had no one stopped me, or apprehended me, regardless of whether I could see or sense *them*?

It still didn't work. None of it did.

In the end I threw away the pad and went in the garden for a cigarette. I only had a couple left. And I still hadn't eaten. I wasn't ready to regroup on the Safeway mission. Maybe tomorrow.

I grabbed the car keys.

THE 7-ELEVEN LOT looked the same. The white Honda SUV. The battered Ford pickup. What had once seemed weird now felt reassuring.

I picked up the bags from the passenger seat and headed inside. Milk. The salads looked old, the bread in the pre-made sandwiches hard and curling. It'd been nearly three days. So I took a loaf of bread—that cheap shit will last for weeks in the fridge without tasting much worse. Then beer. Wine. Chips. A *lot* of chips. Some tins of tuna. Ramen. I was running out of space in the bags so only gathered a small portion of what was in the chiller cabinet. Mac 'n' cheese, a rice bowl.

Enough for now. Tomorrow I'd be going to Safeway anyway. Fuck the Diamond Hardware door and its weirdness.

I went behind the counter and gathered half a dozen packs of cigarettes. Nobody but me around to smoke them, so I might as well steal in bulk. The bags were now full. I was done.

As I was leaving I caught sight of the office door.

It was shut.

That...was strange.

When I'd come here the first time the door had been a little ajar. I'd left it that way after looking inside. Wind, perhaps? It had picked up a few times in the last couple days. Though, way over in the back corner with aisles and the counter between it and the door, seemed like the door would have been pretty protected. Especially with the outside doors being shut as always.

I went over. Considered knocking but then turned the handle. It opened. Nobody in there.

My mind was split perfectly in two. Half sure I'd left the door slightly open, and there was no way it

TIME OUT

would have shut by itself, so this meant something. The other equally confident I'd mis-remembered and absently closed the door the previous time.

I got out my phone—in my pocket since the trip to Safeway, as I'd written a list on it—and closed the door. Took a photograph. From now on I was going to do that with everything.

I left with my bags but without adding to the list of things I owed the store for taking.

17

THE PAD NOW said, in my semi-legible handwriting:

> Diamond Hardware's glass door
> ??? 7/11 office door

Nothing else but doodles and arrows and a large patch of cross-hatching. The page represented exactly an hour's work. The most significant element was an ornate double-headed arrow connecting the two instances of the word "door". It even had a drop shadow. I was running for now with the assumption that I'd correctly recalled my prior interaction with the door in 7-Eleven. If that was true, then both anomalous incidents I'd encountered involved doors. This felt like it had to be significant. It was why I wrote the two things down in the first place. The subsequent fifty-nine minutes with the pad, however, had seen me failing to come up with any idea of what it might mean.

I went out on the deck, drank my beers, feeling like an automaton. Why *did* I stick to schedule and quota? Why was I assuming I'd have an "evening meal", rather than eating at two a.m., or grazing throughout the day? Was it choice? The body has its routines and needs. It gets hungry after a certain period. It needs to void water a certain time after drinking fluids. In my case—I'd always been regular—it's ready to void solid waste within half an hour of rising from bed. It's a machine. An energy source goes in, waste materials come out. Wheels turn.

Did we mimic that unconsciously in our apparently more chosen behaviors, or were our minds and characters actually the same, fundamentally and deep down? I felt guilty about not having done any work yet today, despite everything I knew about its pointlessness. Why was that? Where was the sense in it?

The beers were slipping down quickly. I could feel myself gathering pace in a way that sometimes happened with Leela when we were out on deck putting the world to rights, Emily safely fascinated by a TV show in the family room. There had been evenings, not many, but a few, where she'd eventually come out after eight o'clock to enquire if there was actually going to be any dinner, *ever*—to find both parents fired up on some topic, turning toward her like rabbits startled in headlights, as if only then remembering they had a child.

Did kids recall moments like these? Ominous harbingers of the news that they weren't the center of creation after all? Or were they shrugged off as a sign that sometimes the universe revolving around them missed a beat—or as proof that frankly, it's hard these days to get reliable staff. Did witnessing occasional arguments between us feel like a major disturbance in the force, or were the following rapprochements comforting evidence that normal service could be resumed, modeling a style of relationship in which every straw didn't have to be the last straw?

I didn't know. Would never have a way of knowing. I wouldn't have been able to find out even if all this hadn't happened. By the time those moments started to echo loudly enough in Emily's life she would have left home and be out in the world living her own life. I might even have been dead.

I opened an extra beer. The garden was very quiet. No traffic. No birds at the feeder. No squirrels. None of the anonymous animals—rabbits or gophers, we'd assumed—that'd occasionally rustle in the bushes in twilight. It was easy to believe there were no bugs left, either, no earthworms in the ground. Perhaps not even microbes. Everything felt like it had come to a complete stop, and I realized that in my heart I knew the answer to the conundrum of the hardware store door. Or believed I did.

Nobody had come to fix it. That made no sense. Instead I'd merely knocked the world off a balance point. It had then swung back, to the instant before the door was broken. My stuck-on note was of no importance in this grander scheme of things. I too was stuck, a beat either side of this moment, in an eternal present.

No future. But in that moment, the past swelled.

EIGHTEEN MONTHS AGO. Long-term colleague, down in LA. Producer at one of the entities I sometimes worked for. Smart, sharp, attractive. There had always been a mild frisson. A warmth. One night a bunch of us were out celebrating after scoring an in-the-room season order from a streamer. Over the course of the next several hours everybody else went home or back to hotels, one by one. We didn't. We drew closer. Knees touched. To this day I have no idea why. It could so easily have not happened. We could have continued as good co-workers, friends, a relationship spiced by occasional flirting, so low-key that only dogs could hear it.

TIME OUT

But we didn't.

You can guess the rest. Either you've done it yourself or you've seen the movies or read the books. Elements of life that had gone a little stale, seeming fresh and new. Really, that's all it boils down to, those afternoons in motels and secret glances and covert messages. You can kid yourself that you've found a soul mate—and we both did, for a while—thus opening a door onto some bright and unique and special new life: but it's not. I'm sure there may be people who find the actual best person for them after they're already committed to someone else, but I suspect the circumstance is vanishingly rare. She was convinced of that idea for a moment longer than me, or professed to be, though looking back I wonder if she was simply a little more motivated to get out of the marital situation she was already in.

I wasn't, though I hadn't realized this because I never thought about it properly. I spent three months not thinking about the future, about consequences or repercussions. In a bubble. Caught in one long moment of now, of feeling as if the world was like New England in foliage season, a light turned on in every leaf. Eventually she asked the question: where was this going? The spell broke instantly. That sustained moment ended there and then, and in the very next one I knew the answer to her question.

It was going nowhere.

I loved my wife. I loved my child. Sure, I loved or had feelings for this other woman too, but not enough. Nowhere *near* enough. I had been caught up in something but I hadn't lost my mind. It wasn't just the Emily of it, either. It was Leela. Absolutely and completely. She was where I was meant to be. All this had been some holiday from reality, a live-action fiction, visceral and tactile. But not real. Make-believe. Stupid.

Dumber than the dead dog across the road.

We stumbled on for a few more weeks but on my next visit to LA we ended it, via a discussion in the parking lot of the bar where it all started. I think at some level we both appreciated the narrative roundedness. It was cordial but also sad and a little bitter. It felt like discovering what you'd thought was magic was only an illusion, and that in truth we'd misdirected ourselves.

The currents of work have kept us out of each other's way since. I still thought of her occasionally, but with guilt and a weary despair at my own bad choices rather than any inkling of desire. The only time I'd thought about contacting her (apart from for an instant the other morning) was the afternoon

TIME OUT

I discovered that the show commissioned the day we started the affair had not been greenlit. Scripts had been written but the project was stillborn. This struck me as genuinely funny, in a deeply ironic way, and the fact I'd thought of sharing this news as a joke proved to me how very over the whole thing I was. I'd hoped over time it would fade into a dim memory I could cautiously chalk down as a learning experience, a teachable lesson about how much I valued my existing family. I believed that might be possible mainly because we'd managed to keep it secret.

Though, it turned out, not.

As to how Leela had discovered the truth... I'd spent a while over the last twenty-four hours figuring this out.

On Christmas Eve afternoon she'd briefly borrowed my laptop to search back for an email I'd received over some tedious household thing, earthquake insurance or a long-ago furnace issue, or something—I hadn't really listened, my laptop was on the kitchen table while I did advanced prep for the meal the next day. Whatever search term she'd used accidently uncovered the single email I'd sentimentally kept from the other woman (buried deep in a folder, but still findable via global search) in which she'd strayed just a tiny bit from strictly work talk.

The chances of this were *astronomically* low but I knew it's what happened, because when I'd worked it out I took a look on Leela's phone and found a screenshot of the offending message saved in her photos app. She'd evidently emailed it to herself from my machine, then deleted that email, and emptied the trash, covering her tracks. Smarter than me. Sneakier, too. If she'd ever decided to have an affair I'd likely have remained clueless for all time. On Christmas Eve she'd merely closed the laptop, said thanks for the use of it (thinking back, had there been a tightness in her voice? I couldn't remember) and left the room.

I guess she decided that for Emily's sake she'd hold fire for a few days, get to the other side of Christmas. The packing of a bag might seem an over-reaction—or at least, another example of going straight to the nukes—but I wasn't going to judge. She'd asked a couple of times back then about this other woman, not probing hard, nonetheless referencing the number of meetings we seemed to have. I'd gaslit her. That's not cool. People don't like being gaslit. Especially Leela. The half-started note on her phone suggested she'd been open to us talking about what happened, so the bag may only have been a precaution in case that conversation went badly. And remember, for all she knew the affair

TIME OUT

was still going on. In retrospect the vehemence when she called me an asshole was understandable. Wholly justified. And then some.

What a fucking mess.

Or it would be if she was still here. Now there was just a packed bag in the attic. The potential for disaster, suspended.

AFTER FIFTEEN MINUTES lost in all this I looked up to realize both that I had been crying for quite some time and also that I hadn't actually started drinking the extra beer.

I tipped it into the flower bed and went indoors, microwaved the mac 'n' cheese and ate it methodically. With my allotted small glass of red wine. Round and round we go. The wheels turn.

18

I DIDN'T WAKE the next day until 8:15. Late. I woke befuddled, thinking I'd heard a noise. Lay still, but heard nothing.

I showered slowly, dressed slowly, went down to the kitchen and slowly made coffee, which I then sipped on the deck. It felt as if I was moving through molasses. In periods of wakefulness in the night I'd toyed with the idea of re-checking the area for pets. Didn't seem a lot of point. I didn't yet have an alternative plan.

Maybe some work. For its own sake. Not because the script would have to be handed in, but because it wouldn't. It had been a long while, but I vaguely remembered the idea of writing because I felt like it. Because I had something to say. I wondered if it might be worth trying to revisit that. Seeing if there was a point beyond the pointlessness.

That was the plan until I made a calamitous discovery. I'd run out of coffee. Both ground and instant. I knew 7-Eleven didn't stock either (presumably to drive sales of their own lackluster brews).

Fine. I'd been in the house for a spell. Get some fresh air.

I WASN'T DRAWN to the idea of Safeway. In a world of possibility—however solitary—it seemed dumb to keep running along the same limited tracks. I'd done too much of that, and not only recently.

I headed downtown instead. The lights were red as I crossed Mission but I paid them no heed. Their commands no longer restricted me. No cars on the road. Business as the new usual. I didn't bother to park in an actual spot when I reached Pacific, instead coming to a halt randomly on a side street—though as I got out of the car I realized I probably would next time. The car looked stupid that way. There's satisfaction in parking accurately. Like writing for its own sake, maybe.

Live like no one's watching. Because they aren't.

I walked to the corner carrying our spade—reasonably convinced I'd be able to accomplish my mission without having to drive the car into a door this time—and considering coffee-acquisition options. Several indie shops along the main drag

TIME OUT

were likely to have large stocks of ground beans, though most had a tendency to leave them roast a little green for my taste. New Leaf was a smarter destination: a boutique grocery halfway down the street that would have both bags of roast *and* jars of instant. Though, thinking about it, if I went to one of the actual coffee shops I could in fact take an actual espresso machine. Huh. I had no idea how to use one but judging by some of the baristas I'd encountered over the years, it couldn't be that hard.

Interesting. Probably very heavy, though. A quest for later in the week. New Leaf still made the most sense and as I was turning the corner onto the main drag I rolled my shoulders, preparing for the swings of the shovel.

On the other side of the road.

A man.

I STOPPED DEAD in my tracks, so surprised that I dropped the shovel. It was like an optical illusion. Or a painting. My instinct was to turn and run. I don't know why. It was just…a lot.

Then I heard myself saying: 'Hey!'

Even before the semi-shout was out of my mouth, I realized something was off. Pacific is wall-to-wall stores, trees dotted along it, there's been talk of pedestrianizing. The man was at the far side of the crossing, half a block up from New Leaf. He looked exactly as if he was about to step out and was glancing left, as though to check for traffic, head turned slightly away.

But he wasn't moving.

I called again, more quietly. Waited a beat, then went over to the road. When I say he wasn't moving, I mean it literally. He wasn't waiting for traffic to pass—there wasn't any, hadn't been for three days. He was motionless. His head didn't return to the front after the completion of the glance left. It stayed that way.

I approached. He was a standard Santa Cruz man of middle age. Medium height. Short and fairly tidy hair, brown ceding to grey at the temples. Hands in the pockets of cargo shorts. The top of a black T-shirt visible beneath a zip-up grey hoodie. White socks, sneakers. Hazel eyes. Unblinking. Still glancing down the street.

'Hey,' I said, again. Conversationally this time. Gently. Still no response. I walked around him. All the way around. Looked at him from all sides. A lick of breeze moved a patch of his hair momentarily. There was no question he was real. A person.

TIME OUT

Absolutely motionless.

I reached out and touched his shoulder. The cloth felt exactly as you'd expect. The predictable feeling of bone under two layers of cloth and not too much flesh. He looked pretty fit.

I went back around and moved in closer to look him in the eyes again, trying to gauge if there was anybody in there. His eyes did not seem either alive or dead. More like those of someone in a very good candid photograph, where an instant of time has been caught well enough to reassure the viewer there had been moments before and after, that this was indeed a living thing.

'Can you hear me?'

No response. I touched him gently on the chest. Then a little harder. There was resistance there. He was firmly planted.

I nudged him again, harder, out of a combination of fear, bafflement and frustration. And something horrible happened.

He fell over.

Toppled straight over backward, to land flat-out on the sidewalk behind where he'd been standing. Shocked though I was, I saw he'd made absolutely no attempt to prevent or break his fall. He teetered and went over like a mannequin.

'Shit, sorr—'

He lay there, stiffly. His head still turned in exactly the way it had been when he was upright. With his body in this position it was more obvious his right foot had been slightly ahead of the left, as if he'd been on the cusp of stepping out into the street, reassured the way was clear. It was the same now, slightly elevated from the ground. Unwavering. Neither rigid nor trembling with the effort. Just stuck there.

Absurdly I found myself leaning over, embarrassed for him, convinced I needed to get right onto standing him back upright again. Like a toy soldier. I stopped before my hands got to him, realizing he'd be heavy and unwieldy and also...

...what the fucking *fuck*?

I backed away, watching him carefully. Kept going until I was on the opposite sidewalk, darting glances up and down the street as I went, unconsciously afraid I'd been observed doing this thing. Everywhere remained deserted.

I retreated around the corner of the side street where I'd left the car, where I could be out of sight. From whom, I wasn't sure. The guy on the ground, maybe. My hands were shaking. I smoked a cigarette fast. Didn't even try to make sense of the situation, simply tried to figure out what I should do. Came up blank.

TIME OUT

I realized I'd left my spade behind. Thought about leaving it, but it felt weirdly like evidence and also it was my fucking shovel. I went back to the corner and poked my head around.

Found myself whispering: 'Okay, *fuck* this.'

The man was on his feet again. Exactly as he had been. On the other side of the street, glancing left.

I abandoned the spade and ran to the car.

19

I MADE MYSELF drive around town for half an hour. I saw:

Another man, much older, sitting on a bench outside a church and looking out over their small commemorative garden. I slowed right down as I passed but he did not move his head or blink.

A teenage girl by a beat-up Mustang on a side street a couple roads back from the ocean. Her hand was gripping the driver's side door handle. Her upper body was tilted slightly backward, as if frozen in the act of tugging on a door that didn't open easily. She remained in that awkward position as I drove by, reversed back past her, and then drove by again.

At the end of the wharf, a middle-aged woman standing by herself. I'd parked at the foot of the wharf and walked all the way along it, pointlessly fast, for no reason except my head was spinning and I didn't know what else to do. I saw her from some distance away. Leaning forward, hands on the railing either side, long blonde hair flowing to my left, played with by the wind. I went right up beside. She was wearing big sunglasses and gazing out across the bay, with a small, contented smile.

I was about to leave but on impulse reached out to her wrist. Lightly placed my thumb on the back and my index at a point just before where it joined the hand. Nothing. No pulse.

Though—

Was that something? A faint, single thud, a solitary nano-pressure against the tip of my finger? I wasn't sure.

I SAW A couple more people on the way home. So, about half a dozen, all told. Not many. But when I pulled into the parking lot of the 7-Eleven there were now three cars instead of two. A new-looking Nissan in one of those muted colors that are fashionable. A guy was in the driver's seat. His right hand was reached up toward the seatbelt. It stayed that way as I walked past.

Someone was now standing behind the counter inside the store.

A young Hispanic guy. Not one of the clerks I knew well. He was looking out onto the lot, face caught in a moment of thought.

TIME OUT

'Hey,' I said. He did not reply or move.

I leaned forward and waved my hands in front of his face. Nothing. I watched him for five minutes and then left, thinking maybe I'd been right about the office door the day before.

When I got home there was someone walking down the street. They too were motionless, caught in the act of striding. It seemed like a very fragile moment of balance. I suspect only the lightest of touches would tilt him over sideways. So I didn't do that.

I went inside the house and locked the door.

I WORKED FOR a few hours because I had no idea what else to do. When I took a cigarette break in the afternoon I heard a sound and turned to see a squirrel bounding its way along the squirrel highway, that fence along the side of the garden that divides our property from Carol's. I realized this must have been what had woken me first thing. The same sound.

At four I remembered something else.

I didn't have the spade. Of course it didn't matter. But it was our spade. Leela used it in the garden. *Used* to use it. We'd bought it together soon after moving to Santa Cruz. In Diamond Hardware, in fact. It felt weird knowing it was down there on Pacific, lying in the street. I think I still felt guilty about knocking the standing guy over, also. Or guilty about something, at least, maybe about *everything*, and that's what I was attaching the emotion to. The spade was ours and it was part of the world before and it was lying abandoned on the street.

I drove back downtown.

I PARKED PROPERLY this time. I had seen half a dozen people on the way down. Motionless on street corners. One frozen in the forecourt of the gas station, as if caught in the act of heading to pay or to pick up cigarettes or beer.

The man on Pacific was still standing exactly where he had been, our spade near his feet. I went over, picked it up. Walked with it up that side of the street, as far as the clock tower.

There now was a man sitting outside Betty's Burgers, at one of the metal tables. His left hand was in his lap, the other out in front, thumb and index finger coming together as if reaching for a French fry. There was nothing on the table in front of him.

TIME OUT

The door to Bookshop Santa Cruz was open and a young woman in the act of coming through it, looking straight across the street at the fancy shoe store, as if focused on her next destination.

I returned to the car and headed home. Mission accomplished. World, meanwhile, insane. Just before the last turn into our street I changed my mind and followed Borland toward the 7-Eleven instead.

I did not get out of the car, but idled there in the lot for a few minutes. I could see through the window that the clerk was still motionless behind the counter. The man in the Nissan was no longer in his Nissan, however. He was now halfway between it and the 7-Eleven, frozen in mid-stride. Not heading in the direction of the convenience store, but as if back toward his car.

I DRANK MY beers on the deck. One after the other. The birdfeeder remained empty but I heard a thud and turned to see a cat on the fence. The ginger one. It stared back at me. Turned and disappeared from whence it had come.

I did not know what to eat but discovered the packs of ramen I'd gathered yesterday were all chicken flavor. Unconsciously chosen because it's the one Emily likes. So I had one of those. When I was finished I realized it was Tuesday, for whatever that meant these days, and tomorrow was trash collection morning. Of course it wouldn't happen, but still, Tuesday night is trash-out night. I considered adding the Christmas leftovers to the bag but found I still couldn't bring myself to do it, and so took it outside without them. I opened the back gate and pushed the cart onto the street. The man was still there, still frozen, but now five yards further down the street. I didn't know what that meant.

After that I spent a while with my glass of red wine writing a letter. It got long and then very long and the longer it became the further it traveled from what I wanted to say. I had a notion of what that was, but couldn't find it in words. They will do that to you sometimes. Hide just out of reach.

Eventually I went to bed.

20

AT EIGHT THE next morning I was in the living room with a cup of herbal tea. On the couch, looking out the window at the street.

After long inspection I'd now identified the man outside. A neighbor. From further up the street, from one of the last couple houses before the end. Perhaps the early morning light had helped me recognize him, because I'd seen him in the past when I'd headed up that way first thing for one of my so-called runs.

He was no longer stationary. He started from where I'd first seen him yesterday afternoon. Walked thirty yards down the street, more-or-less to where he'd been when I'd seen him later at night, putting out the trash. His progress from one point to the other looked entirely normal. A man in his sixties out for a walk.

When he reached the lower position, however, he reversed. Literally reversed. Walked backwards up the way he'd come, until he was at his starting point. Then he did it again.

He did it exactly the same each time, and when he was going backwards he wasn't actually walking backwards. Walking backwards is hard, even if you've practiced enough to not need to glance around to check you're on track. The motion is awkward, short-stepped, self-conscious. This guy's wasn't. He was walking forward, just in reverse.

He had been doing this for an hour and a half. That's how long I'd been watching, anyway. Who knew how long before that.

EVEN WHILE I was showering I was wondering why I was doing it, and knew the answer was because that's what I always do. I drove downtown. I parked in the same street but not the same spot. There was a car in that one now. The car was empty.

The man I'd knocked over was still on the crosswalk. That was the same. What was different was that he too was in motion now, in a similar fashion to the man on my street. He walked across the road, taking that little side-glance to the left before he set off. He made it to the other side and then

TIME OUT

went back—in a perfect reverse of his previously forward motion.

He wasn't the only one. I went up the street one way and back the other—at first cautiously, but it became clear that despite the people around, I was unobserved. In all honesty, if I'd encountered this situation the week before, I would probably have lost my mind. I guess the last several days had toughened it. Or softened it to the point of no resistance.

The stores were all open. Most were empty but trying the doors showed they were unlocked. About a quarter had one or more people either inside or entering or leaving. I went inside New Leaf and observed a grizzled clerk behind one of the registers, sweeping a box of organic and gluten-free pasta across the barcode reader, time and time again, in a slow, tidal movement. The machine pinged each time. There was no customer standing with him.

There was however one in the dairy aisle. A woman with grey hair. She wandered to the end nearest the doors, selected a carton of milk, put it in her basket. Then walked along the cheeses as if browsing. At the other end she turned around and—curiously—walked back, but *not* in reverse. Looking almost normal. When back at the front of the store she put the milk back where it had come from. She repeated this five times in my presence.

I went to the aisle with the instant coffee and grabbed a jar. Walked it to the register. 'Can I pay for this?'

It seemed like the guy hesitated for a moment, but he said nothing and continued moving the box of pasta over the barcode reader. Again and again.

I WALKED PAST the man outside Betty's Burgers. There was still no food in front of him but he was repeating an action as if picking up a single fry, dipping it in ketchup, and taking it to his mouth, over and over again.

The woman who'd been frozen coming out of the bookstore was also in motion. She left the store and walked across the street (halting for a beat as she stepped into the road) before going into the shoe store. She immediately came back out—like the woman in New Leaf, facing in the right direction—and returned to the bookstore. She remained inside for a little while before coming out and repeating the entire sequence.

On impulse, on her fourth circuit I stepped out into the street and stood in her way. She swerved around me as if avoiding another pedestrian, and disappeared into the bookstore again.

TIME OUT

Hearing a sound that I hadn't in days, I hurriedly got out of the road too.

A car was coming down Pacific.

Slowly. An elderly woman was behind the wheel. She drove past me, stopped thirty yards down the street, and reversed back past, all the way to the top of the mall. The driver kept staring straight ahead throughout the process, and the vehicle's speed remained constant throughout.

Then it came back. The young woman was coming out of the bookstore and got to the street as the car was coming. I was about to reach out, try to warn her despite the fact she seemed to have no awareness of my presence, but…

She paused for that beat before stepping out into the road. That was enough for the car to cruise past. Though she didn't seem to be actively aware of the car, their cycles fitted together.

I walked back to my own vehicle feeling like a ghost.

21

THERE WERE NOW four people in our street. The original man, the one I'd been watching early that morning, was still at it. His range had extended. He was still going backward half the time, but after making it about eighty yards down the road. He had been joined by a man in early middle-age, standard issue tech bro, on a mountain bike. His loop was about two hundred yards, up almost to the gate to the woods, then back around and around, at about a quarter of what you'd consider a normal speed.

I went indoors, made a cup of coffee immediately—it had been over twenty-four hours—and took my laptop to where I couldn't see the street. For the rest of the day I alternated between working, and smoking on the deck.

By late afternoon I was feeling restless and decided to take a walk. I needed a destination and, of course, beer. I had some left from yesterday's box but wanted something different.

I didn't have to drink the same beer every night.

WALKING GUY IN the road had extended his range to about two hundred yards. I thought the biker had disappeared but then he appeared through the gate at the top and rode down the road, still in slow motion but faster than before.

I walked down the hill and along Borland. Two cars passed, going about ten miles an hour. Three people were sitting at the bus stop that caters for college students. All were staring straight ahead. A woman and a young boy came out of the school holding hands and walked as far as the road before returning backwards the way they'd come.

There were now five cars in the lot of 7-Eleven and a student-aged girl in the laundromat. I watched as she took a batch of washing out of one of the machines and transferred it to a dryer, before then taking it out of the dryer and putting it back in the washer. It reminded me uncomfortably of how it had been with the dishwasher in our house, in normal times.

Meanwhile the man I'd seen there yesterday came out of the store and ambled to his car. He

TIME OUT

climbed in, put on his seatbelt, started the engine. Drove out into the road, turned left and went around to re-enter the lot by the second entrance. He parked in the same spot, got out, and walked back into the store. A few minutes later he came out and repeated the sequence.

I went in the store. The clerk was no longer gazing out of the window. He was taking taquitos from a box and putting them on the rollers. Then removing them and returning them to the box.

I went to the fridge and grabbed a six-pack at random. I still had plenty of cigarettes. I was halfway to the door when I heard something marvelous and bizarre.

'Yo,' the clerk said. 'You can't just take the beer, dude.'

It was the first voice I'd heard in four days. He didn't seem to have a follow-up statement and I hadn't brought my wallet or phone. I continued walking. When I glanced back from the lot the clerk had returned to putting taquitos on the rollers, and the guy outside had parked his car again.

The clothes in the laundromat went round and round.

I walked home the other way, up the steep open hill past faculty housing to a section of the woods a half-mile from the top of our street. Halfway along this there's an open section that yields a view over the top of an old quarry, right across the bay.

On a clear day you can see all the way to Monterey. It was a clear day. Clear enough that, in the far distance, I thought I could see a chemtrail.

It wasn't, though, just a cloud.

22

BEERS ON THE deck.

Birds at the feeder.

Two squirrels running along their highway.

I'd been a little late coming out. Spent an hour out front standing in the street watching. Only one more person had appeared, but foot traffic always slackens in the late afternoon. Didn't see the guy on the bike. The older guy was now turning around to walk the proper way when returning to the top of the street. He went into the house at the end and stayed inside for five minutes before coming back out. I recalled now having seen a woman of around the same age tending their front garden. Presumably she was inside. Perhaps moving from place to place in the kitchen. I wondered if they'd started speaking to each other again, and if so, what those sentences were. Short, to begin with. Then longer, and longer, until eventually you couldn't see the joins. I wondered how long before they couldn't tell the difference—before *any* of the people I'd seen today could. I already knew the answer.

They'd never know.

Did that change anything? I thought it might, to me. But then I realized perhaps it'd always been this way.

As I was sitting at the counter with my glass of wine and some leftovers, which tasted fine, I was startled by a sudden noise from somewhere else in the house. I headed cautiously out into the living area. It was coming from the family room.

The television had come to life.

An advertisement for a pharmaceutical product. The gentleman concerned began the scene looking sad. After consuming two green pills with a name you'd have to be Czechoslovakian to pronounce, his mood improved markedly and he embarked upon a montage of outdoor activities with a very cheerful woman of his own age. This was followed by an extended and quickly-spoken list of the ways in which the medication, on the other hand, might kill you dead.

Then the advert started again at the beginning.

I turned the television off and went and finished my food and then worked for a while before getting ready to go upstairs. Just after I'd brushed my teeth, my phone rang. I stared at it.

TIME OUT

Picked it up, very cautiously. Put it to my ear.

'Hey, it's Mark,' a voice said. It was Mark's voice. 'Merry Christmas and all that. Been a while. Let's have a drink next week. Call me.' Then the line went dead.

As I stood blinking, not sure what to do, the phone rang again. 'Hey, it's Mark,' his voice said. 'Merry Christmas and all that. Been a while. Let's have a drink next week. Call me.'

I put the phone on vibrate and left it on the couch and went to bed.

23

WHEN I WOKE next morning I lay for a few minutes with my eyes shut. Listening. Eventually I turned my head and confirmed what my ears had already suspected.

There was a shape on the other side of the bed. Back turned toward me.

I re-closed my eyes. Waited until I had myself under control and my chin was no longer trembling. Got out of bed. Went downstairs and put the kettle on. Made a cup of coffee. I needed a moment to gather myself.

I tracked down the vape I hadn't used in several days and took it and the hot drink out into the garden. It was a little chilly. I could hear birdsong. There were two fading chemtrails far above, crossing each other.

I spent a while walking in slow circles around the pool. When the bird paused for breath I realized I could hear the sound of distant traffic now too.

Then something else. From out in the street came a big, booming bark, as a dumb dog went haring off down the road, exasperated owners doubtless running in pursuit.

'You're up early.'

I FROZE, TURNED round. Leela was a few yards away, barefoot, in her dressing gown. Eyes watchful. Arms tightly folded.

'Hey,' I said. 'I was about to bring you coffee.'

She didn't say anything. The moment stretched. Her face stiffened. This was a moment, *the* moment, and I knew what had to go in it. 'We need to talk,' I said.

Leela blinked, then nodded. 'Yes we do.'

'I'm sorry.'

She nodded again, more slowly this time.

SHE TOLD ME later—months later, and they were long months, and at times very hard—that in that moment she'd already been able see in my face, somehow, that the situation was over and I knew what I had done and how bad it was, and I was out

TIME OUT

the other side and still hers and always would be, if she wanted me.

But I didn't know that back then, just as I didn't know then whether we'd get through this, or if I'd ever again be able to take the world and its blessed rhythms for granted; or that one day, five years later, Leela and I would sit close together on the couch, sipping wine and talking and laughing while music played and Emily in the kitchen attempted to single-handedly replicate her father's traditional Christmas lunch. And nailed it.

I know that now.

I know all of it now.